THE GRAND MASTER PLAN

THE
GRAND MASTER PLAN

Ann Wolff

Marion Boyars　　　London　　　New York

First published in Great Britain and the United States in 1985 by Marion Boyars
Publishers
24 Lacy Road, London SW15 1NL
262 West 22nd Street, New York, NY 10011

Distributed in the United States by
The Scribner Book Companies Inc.

Distributed in Canada by
Collier Macmillan Canada Inc

Distributed in Australia by
Wild and Woolley Pty Ltd.

British Library Cataloguing in Publication Data
Wolff, Ann
    The Grand Master Plan.
    I. Title
    823'.914[F]   PR6073.03/

Library of Congress Cataloging in Publication Data
Wolff, Ann
    The grand master plan

    Summary: Five-year-old Millie, intelligent, neglected daughter of an English public
school headmaster, unleashes, on the day of an old boys' cricket match, a fiendish plot to
overthrow the social and moral world of the school.

    [1. Schools—Fiction.   2. England—Fiction.   3. Behavior—Fiction]   I. Title.
PZ7.W82123Gr   1985   [Fic]   84-14636

ISBN 0-7145-2827-7 Cloth

Typeset in 11 point Times
by Essex Photo Set, Rayleigh

Printed and bound in Great Britain by
Biddles Ltd, Guildford and King's Lynn

About the Author

Ann Wolff has been a medical researcher with special reference to schools, was a TV producer for 10 years, and now works as a writer and musician. She teaches TV studies part-time and is a tutor of film in Art Colleges. She lives in London and has three children.

About the Book

Millie is a neglected, intelligent 5 year old left to her own mischievous devices in a minor English public school where her father is headmaster. Adults treat her with amused indulgence, unaware of her fiendish Grand Master Plan to overthrow the social and moral world of the school. On the day of an Old Boys' cricket match Millie unleashes the plot that results in her banishment and sends her mother spiralling into madness.

In this outstanding first novel, Ann Wolff brilliantly sustains the consciousness of her child protagonist as she learns to reason and manipulate. Her mixture of insight and innocence, her hunger for knowledge as a means to power and the meagreness of the information she is able to extract from adults, make her an utterly convincing focus for this rich study of the learning process, child psychology and perceptions of good and evil.

For my Grandchildren

1

Millie was a naughty little girl, and this was literally true. She was definitely a girl because on looking between her legs she found that what she saw did not match up with that to be found between the legs of boys. She was little because her head only just came above the top of the big oak table in the hall, where the letters were laid out in the morning. She was naughty because – but why was she naughty? She knew with certainty that she was naughty, and the reasons were extensive and complicated, and this is a story about those reasons and where they led her.

Millie was proud of her naughtiness, and she would not let it go. She would be a nobody without it, and she honed it and shaped it and let it burgeon. It was a naughtiness of wide dimensions, a complex, intricate, delicate and delicious naughtiness, and it spread into all fields. She would be naughty in her bath, holding the soap down under the water so that it softened and wasted, refusing to come out until the water became uncomfortably cold and murky, splashing sometimes, though this was small scale stuff and did not interest Millie so much. Once in the middle of the morning when all was still and quiet in the bathroom, she leant right over the high edge of the bath and put in the plug, then turned the large taps full on so that the water roared and splashed and steamed and swirled and gradually lapped its way up the sides of the bath, when Millie escaped quickly and ran downstairs, then ambled around to see what people were doing.

She found them all going about their business, as she had expected, writing letters and giving orders over the telephone and cooking and sweeping and getting out the knives and forks ready to lay the tables for lunch. She could hear the voices from one

11

room to the next in the large house, but when she located them she found the talk of no interest to her. It was a long time before anything happened, and then there were cries and shouts from the dining-room, where they had gone in with the knives and forks and found the water pouring through the ceiling on to the carpet, and others came running and there were calls for buckets and someone went upstairs and there were more shouts. Millie waited in the hall while people ran backwards and forwards and gave orders and wailed about the carpet, and then she found the talk was about her and they shook their heads in indignation and pointed at her and wailed in outraged despair, and she was led to her room and told to stay there as a punishment. In the long run she found the deed unsatisfactory. It had given her a moment of awe when she realized the possible extent of her powers for disruption, and she tucked this away in her memory. But afterwards, in this case, the effects had not lasted and within two days all that was left of the episode was the large brown stain on the dining-room ceiling.

She could be naughty at mealtimes too. This had more potential as she had a captive audience with the people sitting in their places round the table, but she knew to be careful not to push it too far or she would be sent upstairs to her room. In term-time she sat at the master's table, a small figure on a special chair with two hard cushions to bring her higher, incongruous among the bored masters of the boys' preparatory school. Sometimes they would tentatively encourage her, flicking back the peas that she threw at them, but they also knew that they must not be seen to go too far. They kept a wary eye on her father, the Headmaster, who sat at the head of the table, solemn, isolated and also bored. He was not concerned with Millie's behaviour because a daughter did not play a part in a boys' school and his job was to keep order among the boys and to keep his authority over the masters, some of whom had disturbing rebellious tendencies.

Her mother also had her place at the table, at the opposite side to Millie to make it clear that she was there as the Headmaster's

12

wife and not as the keeper of the badly-behaved little girl. The child's ill manners could be blamed on the governess, who had been hired quite properly to teach everything to Millie, from how to use a knife and fork to multiplication, and who ate with the senior servants.

Two other women had places at the master's table, the matron and the gym mistress. The matron was a stout and dull figure who was in charge of medicines and plasters and who wielded power over the boys because she also had control of their rations of sweets and chocolates. The gym mistress was to Millie a more mysterious figure. She was young and slim and she had long blond hair which she tucked behind her ears as she laughed at the masters. They made remarks to her which did not connect with anything that Millie knew about. In addition, her father would join in these conversations, when he had remained silent before, and even smile a little. Her mother smiled too, politely and distantly, while Matron always frowned on these occasions and looked down at her plate. Millie made a mental note to find out the source of the gym mistress's influence.

There had been doubt at first as to whether Millie should have her meals with the masters in the school dining-room. The alternative was to feed her alone in her room with her governess, but the servants pointed out that it was a nuisance and more work to carry unnecessary trays upstairs for the child, and this now only happened when she had been banished to her room for an extra long spell.

Millie would usually be rude to the masters at breakfast and lunch, sticking out her tongue at them and saying silly things, unless something more interesting occurred to distract her. Once one of the boys, at the long tables stretching down the hall beyond the masters' big square table, had a fit and thrashed about on the floor and knocked down chairs. All the boys stood up and some even stood on their chairs so that they could have a better view, and her father shouted at them and Matron strode down the hall to clear a space for the subsiding boy, while her mother rushed to the telephone to call the doctor. Millie

13

recognized an upheaval beyond her own capacities, and she paid tribute by remaining silent in the dining-room for the next two days.

Another time one of the young servants, acting as a waitress and carrying a large bowl of semolina to be served out by the boy at the head of his table, suddenly dropped the bowl and burst into tears. She was dismissed that afternoon and afterwards, when Millie was slowly passing through the big kitchen, checking on what was going on, she heard Cook speak sternly of the dismissed girl and add that in any case she was pregnant. This gave Millie food for thought, and on asking questions of her governess she at last found a subject on which her governess was ignorant, or at any rate she didn't get any answers to her questions.

The carpet in the dining-room, which Millie had managed to dampen, was the cause of another notable disturbance. It was large and red and covered the floor only at the masters' end of the hall. It had worn patches, and the music master, who nearly always came in late and in a hurry, caught his foot one lunchtime in a loose strand and fell sharply forward. In putting out his arms to save himself he caught the gym mistress round the knees. This in itself might not have caused such a stir, but the boys, who had been waiting for their curried mince and rice, had been watching the arrival of the despised music master, and they now, as with one voice, all burst into laughter. The noise was deafening in the large open hall and it carried on for quite a few minutes while the boys at the back of the hall redoubled their laughter in the joy of the event. The Headmaster did not have the heart to quell the boys, and he would have found it difficult to do as the masters were joining in, and even Matron was not frowning and she had her mouth open in a faint bemused smile, so he waited while the delighted gym mistress raised the blushing music master and helped him to his chair. Then the Headmaster stood up and lifted his hand for silence and said Grace again. He always said Grace at the beginning of each meal, before they all sat down, and he enunciated each word unfailingly in a fine, rich, sonorous voice.

14

But this was the only occasion when he ever said Grace twice for the same meal. Millie herself had been decidedly frightened, first by the sudden precipitation of a solid master, but even more by the overwhelming noise that had swept uncontrollably round the hall. She sensed the wounding mockery in the laughter, and it was from this event that she learnt the power of the group.

Supper was considered too late for Millie in the dining-room, though to the masters it was rather a meagre high tea, and she was served a truncated version an hour earlier in her room, before being sent to bed. Later she learnt to turn this into a privilege and to use it for her own devilish purposes, and her private tea certainly figured in the Grand Master Plan, which comes later in the story, when she had gathered all her forces together.

There were a number of other areas in the school where Millie could make her presence felt, though some of them were so boringly obvious that she rarely bothered with them. She could wander into the dormitories when they were empty in the daytime, and walk round the bleak rows of iron beds and wooden cupboards, pulling off the bedcovers and pillows. She never touched the boys' few private possessions, and the boys always got blamed for the unmade beds, and she was rarely present for the ticking off, so it was a petty victory. She could go into the dormitories in the evening, when the boys were getting undressed and she was meant to be in bed, but the boys were glad to have a distraction at the gloomy hour of bedtime and welcomed her with saved-up pieces of chocolate or pages of comics, and when Matron or her mother came to turn out the lights, or draw the curtains if it was summertime and still daylight outside, she was never turned out and sent back to bed with a great show of anger.

If she went into the sickroom during the day and found a boy ill in bed, she was actually welcomed by Matron and encouraged to play with the toys sent to cheer up the sick boy. He would pass the time by showing her an intricate mechanical lorry, and then teach her a dice game which took ages to finish and which she nearly always lost as she had not by then learnt to cheat.

She could go into the classrooms at breaktimes, and the boys would show her drawings of aeroplanes and model boats cut out of balsawood and tricks with cards, and once she went into the prefects' room and they showed her a miraculous crystal set which they had just completed, and which brought into the room a whole dance band and group of singers, even if only feebly at first, and from this she learnt the possibilities and uses of knowledge.

But the boys did not always welcome her during their classroom breaks. Sometimes they pushed her aside, though not too roughly as she was the Headmaster's daughter, or they used her on the receiving end of the experimental tricks. One boy claimed he knew all about knots, and he insisted, with his friends, on demonstrating his abilities by tying her up to a chair, telling her that they were the sort of knots which magically slipped undone afterwards. But she found that this was another trick, and she would have been very helpless and humiliated if they had not heard the master in the corridor outside and the friends rapidly stood in front of her while the wily boy tugged at the knots. This taught her a lot, too, about how far she could go as the Headmaster's daughter.

There was a new room off the covered walk to the gym which remained entirely unexplained to her. It was a fascinating room with clean white tiles all over the walls and floor which gave an echo and made a shout sound twice as loud. There were neat white channels with water running down them all the time, and curious partitions and basins and then lavatories, more than one, with only half doors, and she thought it was a puzzling place to put lavatories. More puzzling was the change that came over the room in term time. In the holidays, when the room was being built and the workmen were there, she could run in and out as much as she pleased, and she watched the men painting and putting up doors and turning on taps, and it was a happy room to play in. But in termtime nobody wanted her in there at all, and the boys would not let her go through the door, although she

16

could hear them inside calling cheerfully to each other, so it sounded like a play room. She discovered there were some places that were clearly barred to her. Was it because she was too little, and she could go anywhere when she was older, though how much older was not clear, or was it because she was too naughty, and this was another punishment? She decided to collect more evidence before coming to a decision.

She did not want to go into the boys' bathroom, which had a bare row of baths with wooden slats in between, because it was an old room at the top of the house and it was at no time a happy room. Nor did she like the long changing room at the top of the corridor to the gym, where there were countless hooks and everywhere was thick with clothes, woollen sweaters and coloured shirts and muddy shorts of all kinds, hanging down the centre and all round the sides of the room with hardly a passage in between, and clothes fallen on the floor too among the smelly socks and boots and shoes and broken laces. These rooms had nothing to offer. She also kept clear of the bleak locker room, where the boys shut away their bats and racquets and balls and fought over them. Sometimes the battles were serious, and Millie knew instinctively that she would need a lot of allies before it was safe for her to go in there.

She could go into the boys' library, and pull the books off the shelves and leave them lying around. But she didn't keep this up for long. The books were already torn and scribbled over and not kept in tidy order like her father's books in his study. It would be more useful to learn to write and then she could put in rude messages. She already knew the alphabet, learnt painstakingly from her governess, and she could now write her name faultlessly, though there seemed little point in adding her name where the boys had written theirs inside the book covers.

The drawing-room was a productive place, when she was in an evil mood. It was kept scrupulously tidy, ready to receive the parents of boys, should they turn up on an unexpected visit, or even, hopefully, prospective new parents come to inspect the school. Gifts were on display from satisfied and thankful parents,

17

and as these tended to be from places of work overseas, the drawing room acquired an exotic and variegated appearance. This suited Millie. There were lacquered boxes from the Far East to be pushed off tables, there were heavy pottery vases from South America to be knocked over, there were carved wooden tables on unsteady legs to be collapsed, there were tapestry cushion covers from the Middle East to be picked at. The curtains were a woven product made originally for Persian beds, and she had at times satisfactorily swung on them. When in a milder mood, she could push around the row of leather elephants, hide the brass ashtrays under the sofa, pick flowers from the bowls and drop them on the floor, or simply jump up and down on the armchairs. When visitors were present, she would come into the room and hover in wicked suspense, knowing that her mother would find it very difficult to send her from the room without an embarrassing scene. She might kick over a small table, accidentally on purpose, just to show that she meant business.

'Oh, Darling,' her mother would say, with a light laugh, turning to the couple sitting politely on the sofa, who waited with half-smiles to see what would happen next. 'There's a dear', her mother would say most sweetly, turning back with a deprecating smile and holding out a pleading hand. 'Pick it up, now, and run along.' Millie would stand the table up again, and then hover some more with a menacing frown. It was difficult not to be jumpy with her around.

She became skilled at listening to conversations for long stretches of time, and then judging exactly when to break in with a pertinent remark. Her mother would be reassuring some conscientious parents about the safety precautions at the school. 'There are two fire escapes from the top floor, and fire extinguishers on every landing. The doors are kept locked at night, and so are the main gates though the grounds are so large that there can be little fear of boys running into the road, or even of strangers breaking in undetected.' Her mother smiled confidently and the parents nodded. 'The police brought their

18

dogs last time', Millie would say calmly, 'and they went into every room'. Her steady blue eyes watched the parents as they jerked round anxiously and gaped at her. Her mother laughed shrilly. 'Oh, but that was an incident in the holidays. My little daughter remembers everything, you know. We have a skeleton staff then. It could never happen during the term'. Comfort was restored, but Millie had made her point, and withdrew from this round, satisfied.

She rarely set out to annoy the servants, although the opportunities were there. She could easily have gone into the larder, and been destructive with the prepared dishes of food, or even removed some of them. But Cook's response would have been short and sharp, and Millie would simply have been banned from the kitchen for evermore, and it was not in Millie's plan to do anything which would threaten to reduce her areas of possible action.

The so-called pantry contained unusual possibilities, as round the walls there were large fitted wooden cupboards which housed all the glass, plates, silver, cutlery, bowls, carving knives, jugs, vases and oddly shaped dishes and containers that Millie didn't even know the uses of. It should have been a mischievous haven for Millie, and she used to sort thoughtfully through the wooden trays full of butter knives, gravy spoons, dainty tea spoons, fragile coffee spoons, sharp-pointed cheese knives, sugar tongs and scissors for cutting the stalks of bunches of grapes. She was prevented from a close study of the different sized carving knives and forks and metal sharpeners, as these were kept on a shelf higher up. She noted the stacks of flowered tea plates, the delicate matching cups and saucers, the gold-rimmed coffee cups with tiny handles, the patterned sundae glasses. She looked with wonder in the cupboard filled with rows upon rows of glasses, all different shapes and sizes and with pretty patterns cut in them. She contemplated the alternative applications of the large silver dome-shaped covers, used to keep the food on the serving-plates warm. She thought about the countless plain white plates for the boys, which she had seen dropped and broken many times, and

19

the deep wire trays with the plain knives and forks and spoons that bent so easily and kept going astray.

The pantry was in fact a haven, but of quite a different kind. There was a large table in the centre with a homely red tablecloth, and chairs all round where the senior servants liked to sit and chat. They would drink their cups of tea there, and they were quite happy to let Millie sit with them. She was the one element which reminded them of family life in an establishment which, although not childless because there were over a hundred boys to be looked after, bore no relationship to a family structure. The senior servants remained permanently at the school, unlike the junior servants who were hired only for term-time, and they sometimes missed the cosy comforts of a home life. A little girl with pigtails and a pretty frock and white socks and shoes brought sentimental associations for them, and Millie was always bright and cheerful in the pantry. Not only did she find it paid off to be sweet and smiling, because then they grumbled less when she was up to her antics, but she also genuinely enjoyed passing the time with them. They allowed her to have cups of tea, which were never served in the drawing-room except at teatime, and they asked her questions about the visitors and the guests. She told them whatever information she had managed to make sense of from the drawing room chatter, and she listened to their gossip too. It revealed a world which was going to take Millie a long time to comprehend.

The butler was called Hamble, and he sat at the table every morning to polish the silver. He liked chatting while he worked and Millie often sat with him. He told her stories about the war, about the discomfort of barracks and being shelled and wading through rivers and firing guns at the enemy in the dark, and the rotten food and the cold trains and the black-out. Millie asked him questions, because she had a lot of life to sort out before she could get going. There were going to be wars when she grew up, obviously, but she could deal with these now that he had explained them to her. There were so many other things which needed explaining. Why, for instance, had her father gone away last summer holiday and come back with a beard. Why had her mother found this so funny when he returned. Why had the English master come back to school early, before term started. Why had he had breakfast with her mother on her balcony, a most unusual place for breakfasts, while Millie had hers with her governess. Hamble gave answers that were hazy, and they did not help Millie to see things more clearly.

Hamble was useful for worldly goings on, such as sweet shops, buses, aeroplanes and soldiers, and he could help on anything to do with the boys, like cricket, cap badges, locks and keys, swimming and engines of any kind, but his knowledge stopped abruptly when it came to her parents. Indeed his answers left her more puzzled, because why, when Hamble was so knowledgeable on the ways of the world, were there some questions that he couldn't answer properly. Millie found it hard to tackle these strange areas of apparent ignorance.

Her mother was adept at slipping out of answering any question at all, and Millie had learnt that it would be useless to rely on her as a source of information. 'I'm busy now, darling,' she would say vaguely, or 'isn't it time for your reading lesson? Run upstairs and find Miss Ellen, there's a good girl.' But Millie rarely sought out her governess, who could, like Hamble, suddenly turn unhelpful. 'Miss Ellen says,' Millie tried on spec, 'that I won't ever have breakfast with you again in the holidays.' This flustered her mother. 'Oh, I'm sure she wouldn't have said that. What, Miss Ellen said that? Oh, I'm sure not.' 'Ask Miss Ellen,' Millie said darkly, as she stalked out of the drawing-room.

Millie withdrew to her own room, as she so often did, to plot undisturbed. She had not told her father, when he got back from his holiday, about the unusual breakfasts. She held this in reserve for an occasion when she would need something more than usually explosive. The roots were forming for the Grand Master Plan.

2

The holidays posed a problem for Millie, for there were no
school rules to be broken, and her inventiveness was stretched to
find new areas for her naughtiness. Much of it had to be carried
out when she was alone, and depended on discovery later. She
wandered into the empty classrooms and found chalk, so she
scribbled briefly on the walls. She lifted up the lids of the desks
and found that the boys had left workbooks stacked inside. She
muddled these up somewhat, and came across a neat collection
of small model cars. Her dress had two pockets at the front,
frilled with elastic, and she found that two cars fitted into each
pocket. She would hide them in her room for future use.

It was eerie standing in the empty classroom, now so quiet that
Millie could hear the birds singing in the sunshine outside the
window, and she could hear the bangs coming from the
workmen putting in a new door to the gym. Usually the room
was filled with shouting excited boys, or a master shouting
instructions at the boys, or boys shouting answers to fierce
questions, always forbidden territory for Millie. It was hard for
her to believe that the room could be empty, and she felt the
desks still had eyes sitting behind them, watching her all the time.
She walked behind the master's desk with awe, expecting
someone to pop out at any minute, but when nothing moved she
began to find the room merely boring. She opened the drawer of
the master's large flat desk, hoping to find some secret of his
power over the boys, and she came upon many sheets of paper
with columns of writing down one side, which she recognized as
the names of the boys, and with marks and numbers and more
writing opposite the names. She immediately vowed that she
would quickly learn to write, and she would make columns of

22

names, and this would give her the secret strength to carry out her plans.

She wandered into the long corridor, with its strips of light from the few windows down one side, and dark from the heavy wooden doors down the other side. She had not finished with the classrooms, but they would not give up their secrets all at once, and she would be returning again when the time was ready. The corridor was still and empty, with nobody to pounce out on her from the doorways, though she could never be quite sure who was around during the holidays. Usually this was the time when repairs were done, and she might suddenly come upon a stranger measuring the blackboards for new easels, or standing on a ladder mending the light, or behind the door testing the keys in the locks. She waited in the corridor, but the only sounds came from the work on the new gym door, and all the classrooms and locker room and changing room and offices seemed to be at Millie's disposal. She hesitated, as so many rooms were daunting for a girl on her own. Once she had found the English master sitting alone at a desk, looking out of the window, and he had been very irritated when she had disturbed him and he had told her to get out, and she had nearly cried. She decided to leave the rooms uninspected until the rewards were clearer and it would be worth the effort to summon up her courage.

The corridor led one way through two swing doors and a covered path to the gym, where she might find a ball to roll and bounce. But the workmen at the gym entrance had not been friendly the day before, when she had hung about and poked around among the wood and the nails and the tools, and she had come away clutching a handful of sawdust as consolation. The other way led past the kitchen and larders to the pantry, and she might find Hamble in a good mood, so this was the way she chose.

Passing the kitchen, she dropped in to circle the large wooden table down the centre, as she so often did, and there she found Mrs. Hamble, putting away the biscuits from the mid-morning tea in the pantry. Mrs. Hamble was the Head Housekeeper, which was a most senior position, responsible for the employment and good behaviour of the domestic staff in term-time, and ensuring that the whole rambling place, the boys' quarters and the teaching staff's quarters and the Headmaster's quarters and the domestic staff's quarters and every ancillary nook and cranny, were clean and free from dust and rubbish. Mrs. Hamble was not quite as senior as Cook, who held stern control over all the catering and eating arrangements, and who normally was very particular about others using any part of her kitchen unless she had given them orders to do so. But Cook only enjoyed the delivery of meals for a hundred or more, and she declined to stay at the school during the holidays, leaving the planning of meals for the ten or so remaining persons to her assistant. Mrs. Hamble took advantage of the shift in power to prepare more homely teas for herself and Mr. Hamble, sometimes baking scones and fairy cakes, and Millie kept an eye open for these events.

Mrs. Hamble brushed the few crumbs off the dresser and smiled in what she thought to be a motherly way at Millie. 'At a loose end are you this morning, Millie my dear?'

Millie was just a little too scared of Mrs. Hamble to ask her for a biscuit now that tea was over, but she enjoyed her company all the same, and she gave a pretty half-smile and nodded her curly pigtails.

'Why don't you come along with me to visit Mrs. Green?' Mrs. Hamble did up another button of her cardigan and pulled it straight. 'I'm going down to the Lodge right away.'

This was a real adventure for Millie. Mrs. Hamble had never invited her to go on a visit before, even though they would still be within the school grounds. Millie had accompanied Mrs. Hamble on some of the lighter domestic tasks about the school building, but a five minute walk to the Lodge was something different. She lined herself up next to Mrs. Hamble and waited obediently.

'Good girl,' Mrs. Hamble said briskly. 'Let's be off then.' They went out of the back door from the kitchen straight into the wide

24

yard, where the sacks of vegetables and crates of milk were delivered in term time. Without the boys, the yard was quiet and empty, looking clean and tidied in the spring sunshine. Immediately, the two of them were ruffled by the Easter holiday breeze, and Millie shivered involuntarily. Mrs. Hamble stopped.

'Millie, do you need a coat?'

'Oh no, no, no. I'm all right,' Millie said quickly, and she put her bare arms behind her back so that Mrs. Hamble would not see the goose-pimples. Millie was so afraid that if she left for the long and laborious process of running along the corridor and going upstairs and finding her coat and getting it on, then she would never find Mrs. Hamble again and she would miss the chance of the adventure.

Mrs. Hamble did not move, so Millie changed the subject. 'Why are we going to visit Mrs. Green?' Millie smiled to show that she was not shivering, and she jumped gaily for a few paces. Then she remembered that she had got on her thin canvas button shoes, and she was meant to wear her thick lace shoes when she went out, so she stopped and looked around in the hope that Mrs. Hamble would not notice her feet. But Mrs. Hamble was already reassured, and she beckoned to Millie as she continued across the yard. Millie walked smartly beside her, and their feet crunched on the gravel as they left the stone yard and started down the main drive.

'Mrs. Green has had a new baby,' Mrs. Hamble explained, smiling down at Millie. 'It's just a week old, and such a sweet little thing. We must see how they are today, mustn't we? And I'm sure you would like to say hello to the new baby girl, wouldn't you?'

Millie sighed to herself. 'Oh, yes,' she said brightly, to keep Mrs. Hamble quiet, while she concentrated on this further deluge of puzzles, thrown up in another bunch. Babies, she thought, were babies, and how were they new, and why did one go to see them, and were they sexed straight away? The boys at the school were sexed, she knew that, but did they start out like that? Or did they grow different later on? Could she ask Mrs. Hamble? Millie looked at her closely. She was chattering on.

25

'They were so looking forward to having a little girl. Alan is a big boy now, he's already started school, I'm sure it won't be long before he's giving his father a helping hand, it's surprising what a boy can do. But they did long for a girl, and they had to wait some time, I expect that was because Mrs. Green was poorly. Thank goodness she is out of the hands of the doctors now, and the baby is so sweet, you'll see.'

The Greens, it appeared to Millie, had their own mysterious way of choosing babies. 'I was meant to be a boy,' Millie said, remembering her mother saying that they had chosen a boy's name and not a girl's, when Millie was born, and she was called Millicent after the heroine in a book her mother was reading at the time.

Mrs. Hamble laughed. 'You wouldn't want to be one of those rough boys, playing football and shouting and knocking each other about, would you now. And you wouldn't be wearing pretty dresses, either.'

Millie felt the toy cars in her pockets bumping against her stomach, and she hoped they did not show. 'Can girls do things that boys can't do?' she asked, though she had increasingly lost any belief in Mrs. Hamble's ability to give proper answers. Millie thought of all the areas in the school forbidden to her, and she could think of no comparable benefits for girls.

'When you grow up,' Mrs. Hamble said seriously, 'you will have a lovely house all of your own, with a garden, and your own children to look after, and a good husband who, well, who comes home in the evenings.' She looked wistfully down the school drive.

Millie knew she was talking nonsense. Nobody lived like that. She finally dismissed Mrs. Hamble as a possible source of solutions for her puzzles. They walked round the bend of the drive as it skirted the big walled garden and the sheds and outhouses, and they started down the long avenue of dark chestnut trees. Mrs. Hamble was not walking fast and Millie found it easy to keep up with her. Millie rarely came this way on her own as she was a bit afraid of the massive old trees, ever since

26

branches had come crashing down one windy night and she had overheard her mother next day asking Mr. Green to cut the trees down. But Mr. Green had demurred, and the trees still remained, menacing with their fitful power to cause danger.

Mr. Green was the Head Gardener, and he lived with his family in the Lodge at the end of the drive, by the main school gates. It was part of Mrs. Green's job to open and close the gates, but when the arrival of the baby became due Mrs. Green had found this chore a nuisance and she had left the gates open. Millie had heard this being discussed in the pantry, and it was clear that Mrs. Green had done wrong, though Millie did not know what the punishment would be. As they walked on Millie could see the large white gates in the distance, closed across the entrance to the drive, so order had been restored.

Mrs. Hamble hurried eagerly as she approached the little house, and Millie dawdled as she looked round the unfamiliar terrain, so Mrs. Green had opened the front door and exchanged feminine greetings with Mrs. Hamble by the time Millie caught up with them. Mrs. Green looked at her with curiosity, as they had only seen each other before when Millie passed through the gates with her mother or with her governess.

'So this is the little Miss,' she said, and Millie waited to see which side Mrs. Hamble would take.

'Millie came down with me to see the new baby,' Mrs. Hamble said noncommittally, but then she added, 'she's so often at a loose end up there, left to play by herself.'

'Come on in then,' Mrs. Green said, and fell into feminine conversation again as she and Mrs. Hamble went into the Lodge front room. Millie followed, looking round carefully. She had never seen such a small room. There was a sofa and chairs all right, but there was hardly room to pass between them, and all the pictures and photographs and vases and bowls and boxes were piled together on the narrow mantelpiece, and it was difficult not to knock over the baskets and clothes and jugs on the small table by the window. Millie kept very still, not wishing to cause a breakage and seal her reputation for naughtiness so

27

early in this unusual adventure.

'Ssh,' Mrs. Green said fiercely, and they all three held quiet and listened. A strange little cry, like the cats Millie had heard in the long grass, came from another room, and Mrs. Green smiled joyously.

'There now, if she isn't awake already,' she said, and Mrs. Hamble added, 'Aah, calling for her mamma.'

Mrs. Green smiled even more happily, and said, 'I'll go and fetch her,' in a conspiratorial whisper, as if suggesting a midnight feast. She edged past Mrs. Hamble and gave Millie a reassuring nod, as she left in search of the cry.

Mrs. Hamble stood by the mantelpiece, smiling serenely in anticipation. Millie stood rigidly by the table, not knowing exactly what to expect, except that the baby must be specially delightful. They both waited, and Mrs. Hamble said, 'only a week old, and a good healthy cry,' even though there was now silence. They waited again, and Mrs. Hamble was saying, 'I expect she wants a feed,' when Mrs. Green came slowly into the room.

She was holding a large untidy bundle of wool blanket and shawl, with a long knitted corner trailing down. She clutched the bundle to her chest, and watched it solemnly, making tiny smacking noises with her lips as she manoevred past the sofa. Mrs. Hamble leant forward, ready with her exclamations.

'Aaah,' she duly said, as they both peered into the blankets.

'She's got plenty of dark hair,' Mrs. Hamble observed, and Mrs. Green nodded thoughtfully. 'So did Alan at first,' she said, 'but he turned fair later.'

Mrs. Hamble looked more closely. 'She's got something of her father about her.' She turned her head sideways and squinted into the folds of the blanket. 'I think it's the nose. It's his nose.'

'Do you think so?' Mrs. Green gave small jerking movements to rock the bundle. 'She's got her father's chin all right.' She laughed. 'She'll have a will of her own, you'll see.'

Millie stood, increasingly nervous, both scared and curious to look into the depths of the bundle. She watched Mrs. Green smiling and rocking and clucking, and she hesitated to come nearer.

Mrs. Green saw Millie standing quietly by the table, and moved across the room. 'Would you like to see the baby?' She crouched down, holding the bundle against her chest, until Millie could see over the top. 'Take a peep. She's a lot smaller than you are.'

Millie looked between the folds and saw a revolting object. It was still, white, blotched, creased and at first glance it had nothing recognizably human about it. Millie jerked back her head and looked up at Mrs. Green with indignation, wanting an explanation.

Mrs. Green did not move, and spoke quietly. 'Have you ever seen a little baby before?'

Millie shook her head, and Mrs. Green put her hand in the folds and drew up her finger, lifting a tiny and complete white hand. 'Look, there's baby's little hand. She'll grow to be as big as you one day.'

Millie bravely leant over and recognized the tiny nails and the knuckles and the wrist, and then she looked further and she saw the mouth and nose and eyebrows and an ear. As she watched, the baby stirred its head and opened its mouth and gave a croaky cry, and Millie looked up to Mrs. Green with alarm again.

Mrs. Green laughed. 'She won't bite you. I expect she wants her dinner.' She straightened up and turned back to Mrs. Hamble, and they talked earnestly about the frequency and desirability and efficacy of feeding the baby, while the baby itself gave intermittent cries.

Millie had expected more to it than that. This bundle was a let down, and it would take ages to grow to any useful size, even though Mrs. Green had promised it would. However, there was still enough potential, and hints of unforeseen developments, that made Millie decide it was worth her keeping an eye on the baby. She took a step or two in the small room, and bumped into Mrs. Green.

'Can I come and see the baby again?' Millie said quickly,

interrupting their conversation.

Mrs. Green showed no surprise. 'You can come down whenever you like, Millie. And now that I come to think of it, you must be nearly the same age as Alan. How old are you now?'

'I'm five and three quarters', Millie said, with some pride.

'That's right. He's only a little bit older than you. Why don't you come to tea, and you and Alan can play. He's at a loose end too in his holidays.'

Millie's eyes opened wide at the thought of such an unexpected adventure. Then the practicalities crowded in.

'Will I be allowed to come down on my own?' Millie looked from one woman to the other.

'You must ask Miss Ellen,' Mrs. Hamble said immediately.

'I'm sure you can,' Mrs. Green said firmly. 'Why, it's not even outside the grounds. You just let your mother know when you're coming, and you keep to the drive. After all, you're a big girl now,' she said heartily and smiled to affirm the statement.

Millie accepted Mrs. Green's interpretations, as she wanted to improve her chances of getting to the tea party, and she did not explain that the problem was not geographical, since Millie was left to roam alone over the whole grounds, but social, as Millie had never yet been out to tea unaccompanied by her governess. She did not look at Mrs. Hamble, for fear of her spoiling her plans. But Mrs. Hamble did not want to make any decisions.

'Be sure to let Miss Ellen know,' was all she said, before returning to the immediate subject of the crying baby.

But the noise became too disturbing, and Mrs. Green could no longer divide her attention, and Mrs. Hamble agreed it was time for them to leave.

'Say goodbye to the baby,' Mrs. Hamble said cheerily, looking down at Millie, and this annoyed Millie because she knew all about the correct saying of goodbyes.

'Goodbye Mrs. Green,' Millie said pointedly, looking straight ahead and frowning at Mrs. Green's stomach.

Mrs. Green laughed again, and freed her hand to give Millie a slight cuff on the side of her head. 'Off with you now, and be a

30

good girl. And don't forget to come to tea.'

Millie looked up at last and gave Mrs. Green a smile and a nod, and followed Mrs. Hamble out of the sitting room and through the front door, refusing to take the offered hand. Walking back up the drive, Mrs. Hamble gave Millie a string of homilies on correct behaviour. But Millie did not listen. She was far too busy adjusting her life plans to take into account the morning's new developments.

3

Millie was sitting at the table in her room, moving her pencil round and round on the paper, trying to make the lines into an even circle. Miss Ellen had told her to do this, and Millie was determined to learn her letters. Miss Ellen sat at the other side of the table, talking to Nancy Matters, the Assistant Housekeeper. Nancy's particular responsibility was the proper care of the Headmaster's quarters, the mending of clothes and linen and all the sewing required. Her sewing room was near Millie's room, and she had become a close chatting companion for Miss Ellen.

Millie's room was not only her bedroom and her playroom, but also her lessons room and her tea room, and, when Miss Ellen was there, a small extension of the domestic staff's sitting room. Millie found the level of gossip poor, and rarely paid any attention.

'Not that hand,' Miss Ellen said suddenly. 'That's your left hand. You don't write with your left hand, you write with your right hand.'

Millie put the pencil in her other hand, and continued with her circles. It made little difference to her which hand she used, and she had great difficulty in remembering which was her right hand. She settled it once by working out the phrase 'right hand goes next to light white window', but if she sat at a different table, or even if she sat at the other side of the table in the centre of her room, then the phrase let her down because it could be her left hand nearest the window. Now her pencil was in her writing hand, it was nearest the window, and her circles were spectacularly round.

'Aren't these all right?' she said, holding up the paper to Miss Ellen.

The chatter stopped and Miss Ellen took on the air of a dedicated teacher. 'Excellent, excellent. Now do me a row of nice round 'a's, little 'a's, with a neat line at the side. Take a clean sheet of paper and start at the top'. She turned back to her companion, as her efforts as a teacher never lasted longer than necessary.

Millie drew a careful row of 'a's, and being pleased with them, she did a row of 'b's underneath, and then a row of 'c's.

'That's very good, Millie, very good indeed.' Miss Ellen was an attentive teacher again, now that Nancy Matters had returned to her sewing. 'Let's see if you remember the sounds the letters make. Show me a 'p'.' Miss Ellen had early on proved her worth by painting beautifully executed letters on white cards and pinning them round the room at Millie's height. She had also written out simple words, such as 'dog' and 'cat', with corresponding pictures, and she had even included more advanced words, such as 'ball' and 'tree' and 'house', to be ready for when they were needed. When Millie lay in bed at night she could see the line of cards running across the cupboard doors and along the walls to the edge of the fireplace, and she knew them all off by heart.

She ran quickly to the 'p' card and pointed to it, and Miss Ellen praised her delightedly. While Millie was running automatically to the cards as Miss Ellen called out the letters, she was thinking about her afternoon plans. Her lessons only took place in the mornings, and it was a week now since she had been to see Mrs. Green, so that afternoon was a good time to try out the visit for tea. She would tell Miss Ellen that she was going to play with her tricycle, but she would not tell her where she was going to ride it, and if she turned up at the Lodge then it might appear a coincidence. In this way she would avoid any interference.

'Why, that's marvellous, Millie, you know all your letters. Tomorrow we'll put them together and make words. You'll soon be reading, you know, Millie, I am pleased with you. I tell you what.' Miss Ellen did not want to lose a chance to display the glittering achievements of her pupil. 'Let's write out some words this afternoon, and then you can read them to your mother at tea-time. She will be surprised!'

Millie considered this alternative. 'Let's do that tomorrow', she said finally. She was not so sure of her mother's rewarding response.

'Never put off until tomorrow what you can do today.' Miss Ellen had an annoying habit of using sayings as if they were a final law, and Millie considered them most unfair.

'I want to write a poem', Millie said at a tangent, and produced real astonishment in Miss Ellen.

'Oh, Millie, what ever made you think of that?' But then she quickly saw its potential. 'It's a lovely idea. We must start choosing some words, some simple words, that rhyme. Do you know what rhyming is?' Miss Ellen was launched into an area of teaching for which she was unprepared.

'Yes,' said Millie, with great confidence, because she knew all her nursery rhymes. 'Hey Diddle Diddle The Cat And The Fiddle. I want my poem to be a sonnet.' This was a word that she had heard the English master use to her mother, and it had obviously had a good effect.

'My goodness Millie, the things you come out with.' Miss Ellen was genuinely curious. 'Where did you hear that?'

But Millie never revealed her sources. 'One of the boys, I think,' she said vaguely, and when Miss Ellen still appeared unsatisfied she added, 'it was one of the big boys, I expect.'

Miss Ellen had to leave it at that. 'Well now, let's think, what shall our poem be about?'

Millie was finding the subject becoming a nuisance. 'I want to think about it,' she said grandly. 'I'll think about it all this afternoon, and tell you in the morning. You can think about it too,' she went on, to mollify Miss Ellen, 'because you can go on thinking, wherever you are. I shall think about it in the garden, I shall take my tricycle out and think in the garden.' She had reached her initial information target.

'Very good then.' The arrangement also suited Miss Ellen, who had more to talk over with Nancy Matters. 'But let's keep it a secret, shall we? Don't tell anyone, and then it will be a really big surprise for your mother.'

They went downstairs for Millie to have lunch with her parents, which in the holidays was served in a long, narrow room referred to as the gallery-room because it had a small gallery along one side to reach a set of upper bookcases. But in the hall they met Miss Case, the Assistant Cook, carrying a tray with a meal for one, and they learnt that both Millie's parents were out and Millie was to have her lunch in her room. Millie hated this as Miss Ellen usually hung about impatiently and it made her gobble her food. Also it was no different to a major punishment, when she could be sent to her room for hours on end.

They all three went upstairs, back to Millie's familiar room, and her lunch was eased by Miss Case staying for conversation with Miss Ellen. Also Miss Case had made an individual chocolate blancmange in the shape of a rabbit, which Millie adored, and Millie felt so moved as to thank Miss Case, without any prompting, and to tell her that she made better meals than Cook did. Miss Case laughed, rather as Mrs. Green had laughed at her, as if they knew something about Millie which Millie herself did not know, and Millie thought that one day they would tell her, because it was a friendly laugh and they did not make her want to be naughty.

Millie's tricycle was kept in the front cloakroom, and Miss Ellen carried it out for her, across the hall and through the front door to the wide sweep of the drive in front of the house. Millie got on the tricycle and waved to Miss Ellen while she first rode in circles round the empty drive. It was in fact hard to pedal over the rough gravel, but Millie tried to make it look easy and natural. Miss Ellen waved back happily and went into the house, the cue for Millie to ride fast towards the outhouses and walled garden. Millie considered it prudent to ride around casually for a little while before setting off down the long drive, and the paths in the garden were flatter and smoother.

The doorway into the walled garden was unusually narrow, but with care Millie could steer her tricycle through without knocking the wooden door posts on either side. From then on, her skills were taxed to the limit, because the paths were all laid out at sharp rightangles, and it was difficult to turn the corners without bumping into the low box hedges which lined the paths, and it was certainly impossible to approach the turns at any speed except at a crawl. However, the whole garden provided a lot of pathways, and there were many crossroads and choices of direction.

The paths bordered large patches of earth, filled with every kind of vegetable and fruit. There was the well-dug patch, with neat rows of small shoots just coming up. There was the patch with a wide expanse of green cabbage. There was a patch with earth piled up for asparagus whose tips were beginning to show. There was a flat patch where strawberries would grow and which would soon be covered by netting. There were jungly patches, with gooseberries and raspberries and blackcurrents. There was the potato patch, and the rhubarb patch, and the patch with the heaps of compost. Round the extensive walls there were trees trained, their branches stretched out sideways to make the most of the sunshine. Many of the trees were old and rare, and produced peaches and figs and apricots, and they were a particular pride not only for Mr. Green, who pruned them and sprayed them and netted them, but also for Millie's parents, who referred to them when boasting of the premises to visiting parents, as well as throwing in a mention to the vinery and the ancient mulberry tree, though they did not add that the boys would never get a taste of these precious fruits.

Millie cast an eye across the garden to see if anyone was working there. She could not see right to the end, so she pedalled slowly down the side, glancing at the trees and the plants as she passed. It was too early for fruit yet, but in any case she was not out today for a garden raid, though a check needed to be kept for future opportunities. Down at the bottom she met Taverner with a wheelbarrow full of compost. Taverner, the Under Gardener, was a young, laughing man who spent much time, during the term, standing at the back door calling to the servants in the

36

kitchen, and he had even been known to have put his arm round Cook without being sent out of the kitchen. Millie was nervous of him because she did not always understand his remarks.

'Ha ha,' he said as they met on the path, 'who's got right of way then?' Millie looked at the load of compost in front of her, and Taverner gave the barrow a jerk so that the top of the pile slid forward. She put her feet on the ground and clumsily pushed her tricycle backwards, hitting her shins on the pedals and getting muddled with the steering.

Taverner put the wheelbarrow down. 'What's your mischief today?' He came round the barrow and putting his hands gently under her arms he lifted her clear off the tricycle, and he swung her body in the air before putting her down again, finally giving a little squeeze to her ribs.

'It's a lonely Miss, is it? No boys to run after?' He turned her tricycle round and wheeled it with one hand while with the other he led her by the arm. 'When term time comes, you'll be down the corridors, making eyes at the boys, having a good time.' He laughed immoderately. 'Term time's better for both of us.'

Millie looked up at him, and his face suddenly squinted and one eye closed and then it straightened again as if nothing had happened. She stared at his face, uncertain of what she had seen. 'Can you do that again?'

He looked seriously at her. 'What, this?' His face contorted again, and then he roared with laughter. 'Have you never seen a wink?' He did it again, and then laughed some more. 'You will, my girl, you will, you'll get more winks when you grow a bit bigger than you'll know what to do with.'

Millie tried to shut one of her eyes, but both eyes kept closing together, and Taverner had to stop and hold his sides, he was laughing so much. She paused, and came up with the answer. 'Is it only boys that can wink?'

'Some girls wink,' he said, grinning at her, 'but good girls don't wink, so take my advice and leave it to the boys.'

She was finding him good company, so she put up her hand and took hold of his, and he gave her a big squeeze and another wink, and they walked to the next intersection of paths.

'Here's your turning,' he said, and he put down the tricycle on the cross-path. Millie reluctantly sat on the saddle, and turned to give him a small wave.

'Be good,' he called out, as he started walking back to his barrow. 'If you can't be good, be careful.'

That made sense to Millie, as she knew all about being careful when she was naughty, and not going too far, so while she slowly pedalled towards the next junction she contemplated hanging about the garden with her new-found friend. But by the time she reached the intersection she decided that her original plan was still the better one, and she took the left hand turning which led to the doorway.

Before she left the garden she stopped and looked round for Taverner, but he was hidden by the bushes and she could have been alone between the great four walls. She pedalled out and took a turn round the outhouses, in the hope of meeting someone else. The black wooden sheds had their doors mostly open, and she could peer in at the piles of wood and sacking and tools and mowing machinery. Clearly Mrs. Hamble did not rule here, because everywhere was extremely dirty, and the interiors were dark so it was difficult to tell whether anyone was lurking inside. But Millie bravely stopped still at each shed, and nothing stirred, so this had proved to be yet another area struck silent by the holidays.

At last she set out to go to the Lodge. She started down the avenue of chestnut trees, but she found the gravel so soft that she could hardly push the pedals at all. She tried steering along the grass at the edge, between the great trunks of the trees, but the grass was thick and uncut, and the tricycle came to a standstill. She got off and pushed the tricycle for a little way, but this was hardly any easier, and it was making nonsense of her plan to arrive at the Lodge by chance. So she got back on the tricycle and pedalled laboriously and wearily down the whole length of the long drive. By the time she reached the gates she was exhausted and fed up, and less sure that the adventure was such a good one.

She could see no one around, neither in the small garden behind the Lodge, where there were nappies hanging on a line, nor through the latticed windows of the small house.

She left the tricycle at the bottom of the front steps and went up to the big wooden door. There was a black knocker with the shape of a claw on it, but she could not reach it, so she tapped with her knuckles on the door. It made the tiniest of sounds, hardly more noise than a bird would make, so she looked around again. There was a flap in the door for letters, and she could reach this, so she began pushing at the flap, making it open and bang shut. She kept on doing this for ever, so it seemed, long enough for anybody to stop whatever they were doing. They could be on the lavatory, a rude thought but it could happen, and they would have to pull up their knickers and pull the plug and open the door and come all the way downstairs. But still no one came, so she banged the flap a little more, in case they were in the larder maybe making a blancmange? Sewing a dress for the baby? Having an important conversation?

'Who is it?' Millie let go the flap at once and looked up at the face shouting at her from the window. She recognized a crosser Mrs. Green.

'I've come to tea,' Millie said, since this explained everything.

Mrs. Green looked down at her, frowning. 'Oh, Millie Newman.' She looked along the front of the house. 'I'll find Alan for you.' Her head disappeared, and Millie waited another long time until the front door opened. Mrs. Green was friendlier now, and she smiled as she held out her hand and said, 'come along, I'll show you where Alan's playing, and then we can all have tea later on.' She led Millie through a tiny kitchen and out of the back door into a cobbled yard. At one side there was an open shed, with no doors, and clean straw on the ground, and Alan had some boxes piled up. But Millie's attention was riveted by the high wire netting at the end of the yard, behind which she could see flapping, squawking, pecking hens. She had only learnt about hens from books and pictures before then.

When Millie stood staring at the unquestionably live hens,

Mrs. Green said, 'Alan, show Millie the hens. You can give them some feed if you like. The corn is in the cupboard. Don't take more than a scoopful.' She returned through the back door, and Alan came out of his shed to look at Millie, standing in the middle of the yard.

The first thing Millie noticed about Alan was that his hair was cut differently to the boys up at the school, very short at the sides, as if shears had gone straight along each side of his head. Then his clothes were different, thinner and more colourful, not at all like the bulky grey school uniform, and they seemed to make him move more easily. He lifted his whole arm to point.

'Would'jer like to go in the 'en run?' He spoke differently too.

'No,' Millie said. The sky fell down on hens, she knew from the story of Henny Lenny read to her by Miss Ellen, and she did not want to get mixed up with them.

'The corn's in 'ere.' Alan spoke and moved confidently. 'You mustn't give 'em too much or they don't lay regular.' He crossed to a large wooden cupboard built into the side of the shed, and lifted a wooden peg attached to a string, to open the door.

''Ere, 'ave a look'. He indicated the special contents of the cupboard. Millie followed and saw shelves laden with jars and boxes, and on the floor there were cans and buckets and among them was a sack, open at the top. Millie could see the pretty yellow beads inside, and she put her hand in and felt the strange movement as they all shifted against each other, almost as if the sackful were alive.

'That's good corn,' Alan said. 'This is the scoop.' He reached up to the lowest shelf and took a metal bowl with a long wooden handle, and dipped it into the sack.

Millie looked again at the hard beads of corn. 'Do the hens eat that?' It did not look properly like food.

'I'll sprinkle this in the 'en run.' He held the scoop carefully so that none of the corn spilled over the edge. 'The 'ens love it, they gobble it up.' He walked slowly, holding the scoop out level, until he reached the wire netting enclosure. The hens were already gathered by the netting, jumping about and making more noise.

He watched the full scoop while his other hand felt up the wooden post supporting the netting.

'Can you 'old this,' he said to Millie. 'I can't find the gate.' Millie had to move forward, with only the netting between her and the agitated hens, and hold the scoop underneath with her two hands. She waited while he went to the next post along, which was a double one, and worked at a small metal hook. Then he held one of the posts and moved it slightly, and the hens all rushed about.

'You've got'ter move quickly,' he said. 'When I open this, you've got'ter get in before the 'ens get out.'

Millie had not noticed before that part of the netting was in fact a gate. She was no longer safely separated from the menacing hens, and she felt really frightened.

'I don't want to go in there,' she said quickly, but events were moving faster. Alan started pushing the gate, and the hens rushed forward.

''urry up, 'urry up,' Alan shrieked. 'The 'ens'll get out, the 'ens'll get out.' Millie rushed at the gate, to get it over quickly, pushed it further open with the side of her arm and leg and flung the scoop away from her into the midst of the hens.

'That's wrong.' Alan gave her a shove forward so that he could get in behind her and push the gate shut. 'You're supposed to sprinkle the corn, you're supposed to take 'andfuls and give it to the 'ens bit by bit, not all at once.' But the hens did not care, they were jumping and flapping and pecking in one squabbling mass. Millie and Alan could stand and watch them undisturbed.

'We could see if there're any eggs,' Alan said, and led the way to a small wooden hut at the side of the hen run. Millie was glad to get further away from the swarm of hens, and the hut looked attractive, being just the right size for her.

Alan put his head through an opening in the side of the hut. 'There's one, look.' Millie put in her head and was immediately disappointed, finding the hut dirty and smelly inside, and even if she cleaned it out there would not be enough room for her, with the wide shelf covered in straw.

41

'Can't jer see it? There.' He pointed, and Millie saw one white egg in the middle of the straw. It seemed a silly place to leave an egg.

'I'll get it.' He wriggled forward and gently reached for the egg, and he held it in the palm of his hand outside the hut for them both to study it.

'You take it.' He held out the egg to Millie.

'No,' Millie said, but he ignored this. 'Go on, take it.' He prodded the egg at her stomach, and she immediately defended herself by taking the egg with both her hands.

'You can give it to Mum. She'll be ever so pleased.' He cautiously went down among the hens and rescued the scoop, and Millie waited at a distance until he had reached the gate so that she could go straight out of the hen run without more ado.

In the yard she walked cautiously, carrying the egg, while Alan put the scoop in the cupboard and closed the door. He smiled at Millie with satisfied pleasure and walked towards her. 'Mum'll be pleased,' he said, and then his mouth fell open, his eyes widened, his hands opened wide and he stopped, frozen still. 'Oh, Oh, Oh.' he was looking down at Millie's legs. She looked down too, and saw one white sock covered in red blood. There was more blood on her shoe, and thick red blood trickled down from her knee.

'You've broken your leg,' Alan said with terror.

Millie looked closer. 'My knee's bleeding,' she said, beginning to feel frightened, and put out her hand to lift the edge of her dress. The forgotten egg fell and smashed on her shoe, giving a hideous mixture of broken egg shell, yolk and blood.

Millie stood stock still and burst into tears, giving little short sobs, but this was too much for Alan, who lifted his head and wailed. He cried in great gasps and uncontrollable wails, bringing Mrs. Green rushing into the yard. She looked round and summed up.

'You've cut your knee, Millie.' She bent down and picked up Millie in her arms. 'We'll give it a wash and see how bad it is. Don't you worry, I'm sure it's not as bad as it seems.'

42

Millie had already stopped crying and was able to explain the worst part of the tragedy. 'I was bringing you an egg and it got broken,' she said in a small voice.

'Never mind,' Mrs. Green said. 'There'll always be more eggs.' She turned her attention to Alan. 'Cheer up, son. Be a brave boy and give me a hand. Look, Millie's stopped crying already.' She grinned and wagged her head at Millie. 'Alan's always been afraid of blood, the smallest scratch will set him off. There now, dry your eyes, son,' she went on, talking to Alan over her shoulder as she carried Millie into the little kitchen, and he managed to reduce his cries to sniffs as he followed them.

She sat Millie on a chair, carefully took off her shoe and sock, and started cleaning her leg with dabs of cotton wool. Alan watched the operation, leaning against the doorpost and still giving involuntary sniffs.

'So you found an egg,' she said, as she washed off the streaks of blood.

'Alan found it,' Millie said accurately.

'Good boy,' she said absent-mindedly, as she looked closely at the knee. 'It's still bleeding a bit. I'll put a bandage round it.' She looked up at Alan. 'Do you know how it happened?'

He shook his head miserably. 'Her leg just spouted blood,' he said, and ended with more sniffs.

Millie thought hard. 'I banged my knee on the gate when I took the corn into the hen run.'

This upset Mrs. Green, and she fussed round Millie, and muttered about Mr. Green improving the gate, and then she sat the two children down at the small kitchen table and gave them an enticing tea, with round currant cakes and sugared tea, both of which were treats for Millie. Weak cries started from upstairs, a lesser version of Alan's wails, and Mrs. Green fetched the baby into the crowded kitchen. Millie had a good look, but she could see no change, except that it moved more this time.

'We've called her Beryl,' Mrs. Green said coyly, 'after her Auntie.' Millie, not having any aunts herself and so not being sure what they looked like, assumed that they must be small and puckered and messy like the baby.

She had forgotten about her wounded knee by the time tea was over, but when Alan asked if he could try out the tricycle, she thought of the return journey with dismay. Mrs. Green happily had the solution by appointing Mr. Green to bring back the tricycle later, and she left the hungry baby in its cot while she walked with Alan and Millie up the drive, until they could see the corner of the outhouses. She stood with Alan and gave encouraging waves of her hand, as Millie continued on her own to the end of the avenue, and Millie stopped and gave a big long wave of her arm before she turned the corner, and they were finally out of sight.

4

The Easter holiday tasks were in full spate throughout the grounds, when Millie stepped out on a sparkling sunny afternoon. She had finished the troublesome poem that morning with Miss Ellen, after days and days of concentration and bad temper on both sides. It was a poem about a duck, and they had both in their different ways found it difficult and exacting to choose the right words, and Millie decided, ultimately, that there was not much to be said about ducks. However, it did have rhymes, and Millie knew it off by heart, so they both derived some satisfaction from its completion. But the recitation of the poem, planned to captivate her parents at tea-time, had been postponed by Miss Ellen because it was her afternoon off, so Millie now had untrammelled freedom.

Looking out from the front drive, she could see Mr. Green sitting on his motor mower and chugging in slow strips backwards and forwards across the cricket pitch. Beyond the sloping lawn in front of the house, the cricket field stretched for what Millie thought must be a mile, because a mile was a long way and the trees bordering the other side of the field were very far away. It would take Mr. Green a long time to cut the whole field, in readiness for the summer term.

Half-way round the field there was a cricket pavilion, a humble building of white slats of wood with a balcony in front. Millie could see that the doors were open and someone was cleaning out the locker room, where the boys put on their cricket pads. In the summer afternoons the pavilion was an attractive social centre, but it did not now warrant a visit. Behind the pavilion there was an extensive jungly grove of rhododendrons and bamboo, which stretched to the far border of trees, and she

45

had heard her father make jokes about the pavilion not fit to swing cats and the grove only good for monkeys. These jokes were told to her mother, who was bound to laugh, and never to parents.

Millie set out to circle the school building, which was a substantial journey with a long detour round the new wing and confusing cul-de-sacs behind the kitchen quarters, where Millie finally took a short-cut through the scullery and classroom corridor to reach the other side of the building, the half-way mark outside the library windows. From there she could see across the football pitch, with the grass now left uncut and growing fast, to the swimming pond. This was not referred to as the pool, correctly, because it was indeed a pond, dug out and enlarged, with steps and diving boards added. It required regular attention, and Millie guessed this was happening now, because she could see a lorry driven up to the side of the pond, and a small type of crane in action, and two or three men at the edge of the pond, shouting as they waved instructions.

An event such as this was worth a visit, so Millie abandoned the school building and cut through the ornamental shrubs which were tastefully arranged on the slope behind the building, down to the fence round the football field. The fence was a difficulty for Millie. It was newly made, with strong strands of barbed wire, constructed to improve the security for the boys in the school. There were ways round it, which Millie knew, but this was not the moment for another long detour, now that she had chosen a line of action. So after studying the wire, she lay down on her stomach, to wriggle under the bottom strand. The grass was long by the fence, and once flat on the ground she could only see prickly blades of grass and buzzing flies darting in and out, and it required determination to continue. She pushed her arm and leg to the other side, and then her head, and since all was well she gave a final impatient heave into the field. But this was a badly planned move, as she felt a sharp grab at the back of her cardigan, and though she pulled and wriggled she could not get free. The barbed wire had done its job, she realized, and caught

46

her. However, she was not to be outwitted and she ingeniously pulled her arms out of the cardigan, thus freeing herself, though it took her longer to dislodge the cardigan from the sharp points of wire. It was severely torn, which worried her as she put it on again.

She set her mind on the pond and walked into the field. The grass came up to her knees, and she stopped now and again to look at ladybirds, which she knew from her nursery books, and other, darker insects, which might be more dangerous. One, lying stick-like on the grass, sprung up at her face when she bent down, and dropped with a plop among the leaves. The shouts from the men were more distinct, and she could see the lorry backing further round the pond, but she still had half the field to cross.

Looking ahead, she saw the grass move on its own, and she went over to find the explanation. Standing looking down, she could only see ordinary grass, when suddenly a large muddy lump rose up and landed with a thudding squelch on her shoe. She jumped back horrified and kicked her leg to rid herself of the repulsive creature, but unfortunately the movement caused the animal to rise further in her direction, so she gave another wild kick, which caught the moving lump full square in the middle, an unexpected good shot and one that would have brought praise from the boys, had they all been playing football in the field. Now the animal lay on the ground, twitching, and Millie, staring down, recognized it as a frog. The legs jerked uselessly, the mouth feebly opened and shut, and bubbly foam oozed out at the other end. It was a damaged frog, and a totally disgusting sight. She walked away quickly, hoping it would disappear, and found the grass getting longer towards the pond. The crane was clanking down and up with buckets of mud, and the dank smell wafted across the field. Frogs came from ponds, Millie remembered, so maybe a swarm of frogs was escaping from the workmen. She stared hard at the grass in her path, and as she looked round each clump seemed to harbour a potential twitch. She changed direction at once, and aimed for the gate, which

47

would almost certainly have been left open for the lorry.

The gateway brought her to the path for the changing-rooms and the gym, a dead area, so she skirted the gym across rough ground and pushed through dusty bushes to arrive at the first tree of the avenue. Standing at the bend of the drive, she thought of Alan. He might rescue her afternoon and provide strengths which she did not have on her own, and anyway it was more fun with someone else around. She turned towards the Lodge, but she did not walk down the wide open drive, as this was not a proper visit for tea, and instead she kept to the stretch of grass between the row of trees and the old wire fence, which surrounded the run-down and overgrown orchard. She needed an ally, to face the trials of the world, and somehow she hoped to rout out Alan from his back garden shed, and together they would have an adventure.

In the middle of the orchard the branches of an old squat apple tree, some covered in fresh green leaves and others lichen-covered and rotten, all quivered and shook.

''allo Millie. Look where I am.' Millie stopped in utter amazement. Alan was sitting in the tree, smiling at her. The adventure had suddenly started, with a bolt from the blue.

She quickly stepped through the fence, no barbs here, and ran to the tree, holding up her arms. 'Pull me up, pull me up.'

Alan tentatively leant forward, but they were still some way apart, and there were ominous snaps and cracks. 'I can't, it's not safe for two.'

Millie looked at the rough tree trunk. 'How did you get up there?'

'Oh, I just pulled myself up,' Alan said nonchalantly. He swung from the lowest branch and jumped down, and stood next to her. 'I don't suppose you're big enough.' His shoulder was a good few inches above hers, and they silently acknowledged his superior height.

'You could reach the peaches.' Millie remembered her frustration last summer, as she looked up at the prized fruit nodding in the sunshine on the upper branches.

48

'Oh, I 'spect so,' he said, keeping up his image, and then added factually, 'we're not allowed to pick those.'

'Of course you can,' she said briskly. She wanted no diminution in the sense of power he was to provide. 'Mr. Green's your father, you can do what you like.'

'I can't pick the fruit,' he said plaintively.

'Let's go and see,' she said firmly, to counteract the note of hesitation.

'Anyway,' he said with a triumphant sneer, 'there isn't any. It's the wrong time of year.'

Millie was a bit shaken, but not ready to give up. 'There must be something there, fruit grows from something.' Then a blaze of truth came. 'There must be baby fruit.'

'Well there isn't.'

'Show me, show me.'

They stood opposite each other, their feet planted firmly apart, their arms by their sides, watching, as if about to wrestle. Then Alan turned and walked up the orchard towards the outhouses, and Millie followed through the long grass.

They did not speak as they filed past the black sheds and through the narrow door into the walled garden, up to the outstretched tree already netted against the birds. They stared uneasily at the close shiny leaves and the veiled branches, and the tree remained neutral.

'We're not looking in the right place,' Millie said.

'Told you there weren't any,' Alan muttered sulkily.

'You climb up', Millie said sternly. She had seen authority used by her father, and she knew its efficacy. 'Go up to the top. That's where they grow, at the top.'

'Don't want to,' Alan said, as this was unarguable.

Millie glowered with contempt at the boy, at the tree, at the garden, at the long afternoon, and considered putting into effect a spontaneous Subsidiary Master Plan. It would not reach the heights of the Grand Master Plan, as she was by no means ready for this, but a rehearsal at a lower level could be attempted, and might well be useful.

She turned to the nearest patch of earth and stepped over the miniature box hedge. 'What's this?' she said with disgust, pointing to a long row of green shoots coming out of the earth.

Alan gazed at them mildly. 'Could be onions,' he said finally.

'What are onions like?' Millie was surprised. She knew them cooked, but she had not caught them raw in the kitchen, and she had never seen them in the earth.

'Well, like onions,' Alan said, at a loss.

'Could I see one?' Millie said, instantly becoming all sweetness.

Alan paused seriously, and then said, 'I'll show you one,' and crossed the hedge to the head of the row of shoots. He took the first green shoot in his hand and slowly and solemnly pulled it free of the earth, but there was nothing at the end of it except muddy, crooked twists of roots.

'That's not an onion,' Millie said contemptuously.

'It'll grow into one,' he said and suddenly laughed.

'When will it grow', Millie said grumpily, but she was curious all the same.

Alan brightened yet more. 'I know.' He held the shoot up in the air. 'It's a spring onion. I can eat it.' He put the green end in his mouth and chewed it.

Millie watched with amazement. 'What's it like?'

He screwed up his face and said contradictorily, 'S'd'licious.'

'Give me one,' Millie said. 'Please.' She could be polite now that he was doing as she wanted.

He pulled up another shoot and handed it to her, and she took a sharp bite at the end. Her mouth immediately filled with a pungent smell and unchewable leaves, and she spat and spat. Alan hopped up and down with giggly laughter, and she felt her performance was being a success so she gave some extra big spits before offering an explanation.

'That one was no good,' she said grandly, and she pulled up another shoot. 'I'll try this one.' The second shoot was just as unpleasant, but she quelled her distaste and chewed magnificently up to the root.

Alan watched, giggling uncontrollably. 'I'll try this one,' he said in imitation, and pulled a shoot and took a bite, hopping and giggling.

'Come on,' Millie said, pulling another. 'We'll try them all.' She took a small bite and threw it down before pulling up a handful of shoots.

Alan still giggled. 'I'll try this one,' he repeated, pulling shoots left by Millie with exaggerated movements, holding them up and making faces at them before throwing them down behind him.

Millie went stooping down the row, pulling recklessly, leaving Alan staggering behind, and stood up only when she reached the end and turned to look at the wreckage. There was no longer a neat row of shoots. There were still some standing upright, but the rest were flat, broken, trampled and half chewed. Alan came to a halt when he saw Millie stop, and he stared with growing shame at the ruined onions between his feet. He gave a tentative whine and sniff, and wiped the back of his hand along his nose. Millie knew she must cheer him up. Nonetheless, the general result was a satisfactory start to the rehearsal.

'If you come back with me to my room,' Millie called out, 'I'll give you a car.'

'What?' Alan said, puzzled.

'I've got four cars, you can choose.' An even greater gesture was called for. 'You can have two cars, if you like.'

'I collect soldiers,' Alan said proudly, as he walked down to join her. 'And aeroplanes.' He stopped by her side. 'I suppose the cars could be the enemy.'

'Soldiers have cars,' Millie said uncertainly. They stepped over the hedge onto one of the cross-paths.

'No they don't,' Alan said. 'They 'ave trucks, and jeeps, and . . .'

'Sh,' Millie said, crouching down. 'There's someone there.'

'Where?' Alan said nervously, instantly crouching beside her. They could see a movement further down the garden, a man's back in a checked shirt, coming and going as he worked among the fruit bushes.

'Is it Taverner?' Millie whispered.

51

'I can't tell from 'ere,' Alan whispered back.

'Let's go down the path the other side.' She stood up confidently and quickly walked to the other path, as she knew from her previous visits that the bushes hid her on this side.

'Where're we going?' Alan said querulously, following her.

'We're looking for things growing,' Millie said. 'Aren't we?' She stopped beside a patch where there was a row of bare black twigs, sticking out of the earth beside each other to form a long, low, prickly arch. 'Are those sticks growing?' Millie said, puzzled. Then she saw lines of thread zigzaging between the tops of the twigs. 'Do they grow cotton?'

'No, silly,' Alan said contemptuously. 'They put those in to catch the birds.'

Millie looked along the ungainly row of twigs. 'I don't see any birds.'

'Look, when they plant things,' Alan stepped over the hedge onto the earth and stuck his finger at tiny green dots that could just be seen appearing above the ground, 'they put sticks over them, so's the birds can't eat 'em.'

Millie watched his finger. 'Why weren't there sticks over the onions?'

''Cos,' Alan said didactically, 'birds don't like onions, that's why.' He jabbed with his finger. 'Them's peas, them are, and birds like 'em.'

Millie stepped over and pulled up a twig. 'We could feed the birds.'

'Don't do that.' He snatched the stick from her. 'Peas're good. Let 'em grow.' He tried to put the stick back in the ground, and then propped it up at the top of the row of twigs.

'It just didn't seem fair,' Millie said, feebly trying to excuse herself as she returned to the path.

'Birds're evil,' Alan went on, behind her on the path. 'My Dad says 'e'd like to shoot 'em all.'

This did not fit in with Millie's nursery book pictures of birds, and she wondered if all the animals would turn out to be evil as well. 'Are bunny rabbits evil? And what about hens?'

"'ens lay eggs, see. They're all right if you keep 'em locked up. But we keep rabbits too,' Alan went on excitedly. 'Lots of 'em, they live in 'utches, and they 'ave lots of babies. I'll show 'em to you,' he said eagerly. 'When you next come to tea, I'll take you out be'ind the shed and you'll see 'em.'

'Do they eat corn?' Millie asked nervously.

'Nar.' Alan laughed knowingly. 'You pick green stuff for 'em.'

'Would they eat this?' They were beside the piled earth of the asparagus bed, and Millie stepped across and pulled at one stiff green stem which stuck out at the top of the pile. It was hard to break, and when it did give way she stumbled backwards.

'Cor,' Alan said, watching her. 'Them's special, them's 'sparagus.'

She carried the hard green shoot back to him. 'Can you eat it?' They both looked at the unappetising shoot, and she cautiously nibbled the end.

'I dunno,' he said, curious. 'Let me try.' He took the shoot from her, dug in his teeth and then spat to one side. 'It's not ripe,' he concluded.

'I'll try another one.' Millie went back to the earthen pile and pulled out the next green shoot. She gave it a hard squeeze and then called to Alan, 'I think this one's not ripe either.' She glanced anxiously towards the fruit bushes. 'I know, I'll pick them all, and then we can take them away and see which ones are ripe.' She began tugging at each shoot down the row.

'Millie,' Alan said, worried. 'You shouldn't take 'em all.'

'I can't anyway,' Millie said, out of breath. 'Some of them are too tough.'

'Come away now,' Alan said with mounting fear. 'That's enough.'

'All right.' She had in any case almost reached the far end of the pile of earth. She held in her arms an untidy bundle of pale green sticks, some nearly white, some with earth still on them and some only short stubs. The sound of hammering started from behind the bushes, and she galvanized into action, leapt over the hedge and ran up the path, clutching her bundle.

53

'Quick,' she said in a hoarse whisper. 'Follow me.'

Alan ran behind her, again beginning to whine. They ran out of the garden and followed the path as it curved round in front of the herbaceous border, and there they paused while Millie surveyed the scene. On the other side of the path there were neat rose beds, still pruned and tidy from the winter, and then there stretched the vast expanse of the cricket field to the small white pavilion at the other side. There was no hope of reaching the dark grove behind the pavilion. Mr. Green was still on his mower, slowly crossing the length of the field. To the left the drive broadened out in front of the house, wide enough for cars to turn and follow the drive back round the school building. Behind them the path led to the outhouses and the kitchen yard. They would have to go straight on.

'We'd better walk this way,' Millie said less confidently, starting up the path and trying to minimise her illicit bundle by clutching her arms tightly across her chest. Alan's whimpering was becoming tiring, but he still followed her. 'We can look at the flowers.' The path ran in front of the long border, the full length of the outside wall of the garden. Once out of the protection of the wall, there was an ominously wide open stretch before the path skirted a group of trees and reached the small wood at the edge of the cricket field. It was a long walk for the two of them, and Millie chattered to keep up their spirits.

'Do you know the story of Hansel and Gretel? Miss Ellen read it to me. The two children go into the wood and when they get tired they lie down and the birds put leaves over them to keep them warm.' They were approaching the first few trees, and with the prickly grass and nettles and sticks and the evil birds, there seemed no way of matching up life to the story. 'They'd stolen some bread and they made it into crumbs and this is what they used to find the way.' The asparagus was never going to show them the way to anywhere.

'Where were they going, in the story?' Alan asked, more cheerfully.

'I can't remember now. But they end up at a witch's house and

54

it was all made of sweets, every bit of it, and cake and jam and cream and . . .'

'Wow.' Alan waved his arms jubilantly. 'Wouldn't it be great if we found one of those 'ouses.'

Millie looked at him sadly. 'But it isn't real.'

'Well, not really,' Alan admitted. 'But it'd be great all the same.'

They entered the shade of the trees and Millie left the path to find thick cover. The path led eventually to a gate, opening onto the road, and never, not in any circumstances, had Millie considered leaving the grounds by herself. This would need much more preparation. Now she sought a hidden and private spot where she and Alan could rest and review their spoils. The undergrowth between the school field and the high fence bordering the road was thick and unkempt, an abandoned area, and progress was difficult. They were knocked by branches and scratched by brambles, and Alan complained bitterly and almost refused to go further. But Millie insisted that they must find a bush that would encircle them and hold them safe, even though such a bush was not in sight. Finally she compromised at a holly bush. At least it was dark and hid them from one side, though it was not ideal and it was particularly uncomfortable sitting down on the ground beneath it. She laid out the battered asparagus sticks in a row in front of them, and they looked at them in dismay. The pale, uneven sticks appeared insignificant and ridiculous on the dark and dusty ground beneath the bush.

'You can't eat them,' Alan said, his voice quavering. 'That's certain, you can't eat them.'

'I'm going to try, in any case,' Millie said belligerently. Had she struggled and survived such an afternoon, all on account of some inedible sticks? But the asparagus by now was covered in dirt and shared no resemblance to food, and although she picked up each one in turn, her attempts to bite them were merely notional, and by the end she did not even pretend that the stick reached her mouth.

Alan now was crying in earnest, long wails followed by

sobbing gasps. In the wood, surrounded by tall trees and mysterious thickets and dried leaves, the wails seemed to get lost and become ineffectual. Millie moved forward on her hands and knees until she could see round the side of the holly bush and she had a view of the cricket field. Mr. Green had stopped on his mower half way across the field, and he was twisted round on the metal seat to look behind him, where Taverner was approaching from the garden side of the field. Taverner came up and stood beside Mr. Green, apparently talking, but they did not gesture, nor look towards the trees, nor appear perturbed, so they could be discussing any subject. Taverner then turned and walked back towards the garden, and Mr. Green started his mower and drove directly to the pavilion, where the mower was housed in the summer.

Millie wriggled back to Alan. 'Taverner's been talking to your father,' she stated factually.

Alan sobbed helplessly. 'I wanna go home.'

Millie considered this proposition. 'Perhaps you'd better then.' She did not know what was going to happen, but the rehearsal had been her own, and she must face the consequences alone. It had been fun having Alan with her, but she did not want to irretrievably damage their friendship, and it would be better for both of them if they separated now. Alan's presence might make her punishment worse, and she preferred to receive whatever was due to her in her own way.

'You'd better go home,' Millie said with resignation. 'I'm going to stay here,' she added firmly.

Alan sobbed and sniffed, and crashed away through the undergrowth without looking back. Millie waited until she could no longer hear any sound from him, not even the snap of a twig, and then she wriggled back to her look-out over the cricket field. She could not see the long side-path from her position, so she did not know how Alan was returning, whether he was running or shuffling or even whether he had stopped crying. She could see nobody whatsoever in her whole field of view. She could see the strips of grass a different coloured green where they had been freshly cut, she could see large birds fly down to the grass and hop around and fly away again. She could hear smaller birds chattering on the branches near her, and she could hear the cars passing on the road, and ocassionally she could hear raised voices coming from the direction of the school building. But otherwise nothing happened, nothing else whatsoever. She sat in the same place for a long time, and it began to get chilly.

She tried to study the birds and find out what they did with their afternoon, and she chose a small brown bird and watched it closely while it jumped and chirped and fluttered. But it quickly flew away and disappeared out of sight, and when the next brown bird appeared it was hard to tell whether it was the same one back again or a new one, which posed a problem since she had meant to study the afternoon in the life of one brown bird but if they all looked alike then she would have to extend the study to include all brown birds.

Glancing after a bird as it flashed away, she caught sight of a small figure in the far distance, walking slowly on the sloping lawn in front of the house, and she at once stiffened and a peculiar shiver went up her back. She had for a moment forgotten about the purpose of her sitting crouched in the undergrowth at the furthest border of the school grounds. Now she watched the figure, and she soon realized that it was her father. He was ambling across the lawn, looking down at the grass. It was not immediately obvious in which direction he was going. However, once he had reached the edge of the cricket field he chose a path towards the centre, and walked on with slow measured steps. Millie knew this walk well. It was the Headmaster's walk, and she had seen it used when he approached any group of boys, in the corridors or in the classrooms or on the playing fields, it was a walk that never deflected and never hurried, that was firm and purposeful and authoritarian. Now that Millie came to think of it, she had never seen him walk in any other way. He had his hands in his trouser pockets, dark grey trousers as always, and his brown tweed jacket was open at the front and pushed back behind his arms.

57

Millie could just see the dark line of his tie against his white shirt, the school tie which he always wore with the school crest on it, an inexplicable unicorn's head rising above the rays of the sun all in gold. It had something to do with the Latin motto, she had been told.

It was still not absolutely clear where he was going. He could be aiming for the pavilion, to check the state of the locker-rooms, or he could even be going to the pitch itself to examine the condition of the ground. Of all the necessary activities in the boys' school, it was cricket that her father enjoyed the best. He had been known to laugh and joke with the boys as they waited their turn to bat, and he engineered excuses to join in the game himself by fixing a long series of matches, Masters v. Boys, School v. Old Boys, School v. Parents, and, the wildest of all, Masters v. Visiting Ladies, providing him with the unquestionable opportunity to show off his physical prowess which otherwise would have remained sadly hidden.

The only other occasion when Millie had been aware of her father enjoying himself was at prize-giving. He had stood on the platform at one end of the gym, the only room large enough to hold all the chairs and boys and visitors, and boomed out a welcoming speech in his rich sonorous voice. He was wearing his black gown, brought out only on public occasions, and he was with other important and well-dressed persons, all elderly and unidentified to Millie. The boys who were to receive prizes sat in the front row, giggling and whispering with anticipation, and after short and serious speeches from the other persons on the platform, received with appreciative applause from the visitors, the restless boys went up to the platform one by one, going up by the steps at one side, and down the steps at the other. Between the steps, each one had to smile and shake a hand, smile and receive a book, which had the school crest specially stamped on the front cover, and shake the Headmaster's hand. It was her father's delighted smile which riveted Millie's attention. He smiled, and bent over and spoke quietly to the boy, and straightened and patted the boy's back, and smiled again. Millie had the impression that he was delighted to see the boy go, then he could wash his hands of another recalcitrant individual and turn his attention again to younger and more unformed scholastic material. Her father did not appear as a man chosen to be Headmaster by vocation, but rather as a man doing a job and seen to be doing it well. If a job is worth doing, it is worth doing well, as Miss Ellen would say.

Her father did not go to the pavilion, nor did he stop at the cricket pitch in the centre of the field, but he carried straight on, and now that he was more than half-way across the field Millie had to seriously consider his possible objectives. He was just near enough for her to see that he was not smiling, though on the other hand he did not look particularly angry. He still kept on at his even pace, hands in pockets, shoulders back, head erect, looking round as if inspecting the weather. But the weather was changeless, no spring breeze, the sunshine steady though now weakening in the late afternoon. Millie had to admit to herself that if he continued in the same direction he would arrive at the very spot in the bordering bushes where she was hiding, and this would be a remarkable coincidence, because although she knew that at some stage she must face retribution, she could not think how they could know her hiding-place so accurately. She ruled out the chances of Alan giving a coherent report, and in any case it would take much longer for information to pass from Alan through Mr. Green and all the way through the ramifications of the school building to the Headmaster. Her father seemed to know, by his unswerving manner, what had been going on all the time. Perhaps he knew everything from the very start of the rehearsal, when she had stood in front of the peach tree in the garden, and he had let her carry on simply so that she could receive her just punishment.

It was certainly right that it was her father coming to fetch her, the Headmaster and supreme authority. She would have been very cross and humiliated if a lesser person had been sent out to find her, such as Miss Ellen or Nancy Matters, in fact she would not have bothered to have kept hidden and then she would have had to have found more dreadful deeds to complete her rehearsal, which would have been extra tiresome. As it was, she had the satisfaction of knowing that whatever the worst was that could happen, she was now going to meet it. She could not think what it would be. It would not be a beating, because, although her father allowed the masters to use the cane, he himself was strongly opposed to corporal punishment and believed that order could be maintained by the influence of the personality alone. Millie had quite a hankering for the cane, ever since she passed the open door of a classroom where all the boys at their desks were rocking from side to side and shouting with laughter, and the master in front was also laughing as he swung down a cane, and even the boy leaning over a chair beside the master and giving out mock yells, did not seem too distressed. It looked to Millie like one of the best games she had ever seen, and she was sorry she could not play it too.

The only punishment Millie had ever received was being sent to her room, and she hoped this time they could think of something better than that. She knew how to pass time in her room, with or without Miss Ellen, and it was a tedious prospect. If only they could think of something interesting, like being chased by a giant or sent to a witch's house or even turned into a beautiful swan. But these things only happened in stories.

Her father walked up to the holly bush. 'Come along, Millie. It's teatime now.' He spoke with an even voice, stern and purposeful, stamping his personality on the situation. There was a slight inflection of offendedness, a hint of what-I-have-to-suffer, but the general effect was of well-meant kindliness. He stood by the trees, his hands in his pockets, a man of infinite patience, specially when he was stamping his personality.

Millie came out of the undergrowth and stood by her father. Her knees and hands were black, her torn cardigan was crooked and dirty, and there were bits of dusty leaves and twigs in her hair.

'You need to wash you hands before tea,' her father commented, trying to relieve the situation with a slight joke.

Millie could tell when her father was making a joke because then his head tilted to one side and the corners of his mouth strained down, and if he thought the joke was a very good one, then he jingled the money in his pocket. There was a short jingle now, as he turned away from the bushes. 'Come on now, we'll go back to the house.' He walked at a leisurely pace, so that Millie could easily keep up with him, and he still looked round and about.

'It's going to be a good summer this year, the swallows are returning early.' He loved sharing his fund of knowledge, and the main purpose of children in his view was as recipients of his vast store of facts. 'They'll be building their nests again in the eaves of the tool sheds.' He was always careful to be accurate, and he would never say 'roof' if he meant 'eaves.' Sometimes Millie would try to please him and make a big effort to understand the subject without asking too many questions, but now she was far too exhausted to give any attention to what he was saying. She was so tired that she stopped wondering when her punishment would come, and she concentrated on the long slow walk across the full length of the cricket field.

They walked in silence for much of the way, until they were near the path from the garden. 'Good night, Sir,' a voice called, and they saw Taverner give a sturdy wave of his arm as he walked towards the kitchen yard.

Her father gathered himself together and raised his hand and his voice. 'Ah, good night, Taverner, good night.' Then he returned his hand to the comfort of his pocket again, and they continued towards the front lawn. 'I like Taverner,' Millie said truthfully.

'Do you know Taverner?' her father said, surprised.

'Yes,' Millie said. 'Of course I do.' Perhaps her father knew nothing of what went on, nothing at all. 'I met him in . . .' But then she hesitated. It was too soon to refer to the tender subject of the garden. It would be better to meet her punishment first.

Her father did not pursue the subject either. 'Here we are,' he said heartily, as they reached the front drive. 'With a good appetite, I'm sure, after that long walk.' He tilted his head, but

61

did not jingle money. When they got to the front door, he said, 'you go to the cloakroom and have a good wash. I'll be waiting for you in the drawing-room.'

This must be it, Millie thought, with some excitement, as she reached up to the basin and turned on the taps and splashed water as efficiently as she could over her dirty face and hands. She found a small towel and dried herself quickly, straightened her dress, composed her features and walked to her fate in the drawing-room.

'Darling, there you are.' Her mother was sitting on the sofa, smiling radiantly and holding out her arms. 'We were so worried about where you'd got to. Come over here, my sweet.' Her smile dropped as Millie got nearer. 'But my goodness, darling, your hair is full of leaves. Where have you been?' Millie stood at her knees as she vaguely picked at Millie's hair. 'Do go and ask Miss Ellen to give it a good brush. But of course,' she said, and gave a shriek of laughter, 'it's her afternoon off.' She gave a dismissive flick to Millie's pigtails. 'Never mind, darling. We can start tea now that you're here.'

Millie's father had been standing all this time behind an elegant mahogany upright chair, waiting to sit down at the round table where tea was laid out. It was the full holiday drawing-room tea-time spread, with the hand-embroidered table-cloth, the rosebud china tea service, the silver teapot, polished by Hamble, the slices of bread and butter, both brown and white, the bowls of strawberry jam and honey, the chocolate biscuits arranged in a neat criss-crossing tier, and the currant cake specially baked by Mrs. Hamble and served on a raised cake stand with a paper doily. Millie slowly went to her place and sat on the rush-seated chair kept for her use. It was the highest chair available in the drawing-room, and as the round table was low, it was deemed unnecessary to add a cushion. Nevertheless, her chin was not far above the top of the table, and she looked through the jungle of tea cups, milk jugs, jam spoons, sugar bowls, cake slices and plates of stacked food, and a rising sense of horror came over her. Perhaps her punishment was to be that she was to have no

62

punishment, that her deeds were to go unrecognized, that no reference would be made to anything that she had done, whether good or bad, and that all her efforts had been wasted. A mantle of gloom settled over her, and she stared sulkily at her plate.

Her mother was pouring out tea, and talking to her father about the smell from the swimming pond. Millie was allowed weak tea, or more precisely milk with a flavour of tea in it, and her cup was put down before her. Then the plate of bread and butter was held in front of her.

'Brown or white, darling?' her mother said coaxingly. 'Take whichever you want.' Then, when Millie still stared at her plate, she said, 'brown is always better for you, of course.'

'Take a slice of bread, Millie,' her father said, irritability creeping into his voice.

'I don't want bread and butter,' Millie said, looking down.

'Oh, but you should always start with bread and butter,' her mother cried.

'Have some bread with honey,' her father said, trying his best to settle the dilemma.

'I want a chocolate biscuit,' Millie said. This solution was grasped at, and her father offered her the plate of biscuits. They were long, finger-shaped biscuits, some wrapped in patterned silver paper, and Millie chose a red-wrapped biscuit from the bottom of the pile and pulled it out. The carefully constructed tier immediately collapsed, and biscuits fell across the table.

'Oh darling,' her mother gasped. 'What a mess.'

'Millie, put that biscuit back.' Her father was viciously stamping his personality. He put the plate down, picked up the loose biscuits from the table and replaced them higgledy-piggledy on the plate. 'Now, put that biscuit back on the plate. You must learn to take the one that is nearest to you and on the top of the pile.'

Millie held her biscuit very tightly in her fist. It crossed her mind that the chocolate would soon melt.

'Oh, darling,' her mother said, now talking to her father. 'Don't bother her. It doesn't really matter now.'

63

'That is the root cause of the trouble.' When her father was angry he articulated each word separately, and he was now extremely angry, leaning over and pointing a finger at her mother. 'If you make a rule, for whatever reason, and it should be a good reason, and seen to be a good reason, then that rule must be enforced, and seen to be enforced, with- -out- -ex- -cep- -tion.' He spat out each articulated syllable.

'But darling,' her mother slipped in during the pause. 'That may be all right for the boys . . .'

'Are you implying that I do not know my job?' Her father gave a majestic pause, and her mother fluttered in with, 'but dear, but dear . . .'

'Are you suggesting that I do not understand the proper use of authority?'

'But dear, but dear . . .'

'Are you saying that I am not capable of implementing the fruits of my experience?'

'But dear, you must see . . .'

He held the edges of the table for his final onslaught. 'You -si- -lly- -wo- -man.' Millie tried to make herself become invisible, and her father caught sight of her out of the corner of his eye.

'Millie, go to your room,' he said automatically, and then he felt obliged to add, 'and stay there until you have learnt how to behave.'

Millie slipped down off her chair and, still clutching her biscuit, started round the table, choosing to go behind her mother, rather than her father, to reach the door.

'You poor darling, you must be hungry,' her mother said, twisting round in her chair to hold out her arms. Her mother always managed to look elegant, and now she looked supremely suave, with her loose blue blouse matching the blue of her eyes, and the folds of her pleated skirt falling over her knees, tucked together sideways, but revealing her neat ankles and slim feet in their court shoes under the chair. At the same time, she frequently managed to look distraught, and she gave this impression now, by the helpless waving of her arms, and by the strands of her hair, which was fair and curly like Millie's but held back by an untidy bun instead of pigtails, falling uncontrolled over her forehead. 'I know,' she said, delighted at discovering a brilliant solution. 'Take some of these.' She leant forward, gathered up a handful of chocolate biscuits and held them out over the back of the chair.

'Millie is to go without tea,' her father said grimly. But Millie did not need any prompting from her father. She loftily ignored the proffered biscuits and her mother and her father and the spread of tea, and she stalked grandly from the room, rather spoiling the effect at the end by slamming the door behind her much harder than intended, and alarming herself with the resounding crash.

Back in her room she put the crushed and broken biscuit on the table and realized that she was indeed very hungry. With nothing to be lost, she sat down and yelled, systematically, taking deep breaths and putting in broken sobs now and again so that she could claim, if challenged, that she was crying. But she knew, and anyone listening must know, that she was yelling for attention.

At long last the door flung open and Nancy Matters looked in.

'For heaven's sake, what a dreadful noise. Do stop it at once.' But even Nancy Matters, who had no concern with children, realized that something was up. 'What is it that you want?'

'They wouldn't let me have any tea,' Millie said in a pathetic voice.

'You poor thing,' Nancy said at once, and then had second thoughts. 'There must have been a reason for it.'

Millie gave convincing little sobs and sniffs. 'They said I had to eat my bread and butter first. But I wanted chocolate biscuits.' Nancy would never approach her parents to check such a story.

'Well I don't know.' This was outside Nancy's jurisdiction, but she was not unsympathetic. 'Let me see what I can do.' She disappeared, closing the door, and Millie waited for an endless, empty, hungry age before the door re-opened and Miss Case came in carrying a tray and laughing more than usual.

'There you are, you wicked girl, this is more than you deserve.' She put the tray down on the table. 'Now don't go telling anyone that I've brought you some tea because I'm not really supposed to.' She brushed with her hand over Millie's dusty hair and cardigan. 'But there's no reason to let you go hungry. My goodness, you need someone to care for you.' She pointed to the tray. 'I found some left-over trifle, and I've made jam sandwiches, and there's a slice of currant cake left from the tea downstairs.' She laughed again, and squeezed Millie on the shoulder. 'So you're not doing too badly after all.'

Millie nodded in silent and humble gratitude, looked up at Miss Case with a truly happy smile, and then fell on the food and devoured every crumb, drop and spoonful, thus showing her genuine pleasure in the best way possible.

Afterwards, replete and alone, Millie made some rules of her own. Never carry out a spontaneous rehearsal without a proper research of the area. Never put a Subsiduary Plan into action unless the confederates are of proven loyalty. And prior to the time for action, establish the relative positions of the outlying forces and take into account the repercussions on neutral participants. These were not her words, because she had not learnt them yet, but they were most certainly her intentions.

5

On the first day, the boys returning for another term were delivered to the school entrance by the gym, thus discharging them into the corridor by the locker-room. They could then conveniently put away their new bats and boots, and exchange news at leisure. They knew their way around, these boys did, calling to their friends as they swung in with their bags, and they might show off with a confident swagger if their parents were lingering outside before returning to their car in the drive.

Matron was always at the entrance to welcome the boys and available, if necessary, for reassuring words to uneasy parents. She had a plump and homely figure, and a stern expression, which was just what was needed to give confidence to nervous parents when they were abandoning their offspring. Matron was happy to see the boys again, as they brought order and purpose into her life. She was confused and at a loss in the holidays, and with the boys back she could return to the comfortable structure of getting-up-time, bath-time, breakfast-time, sickroom visits, surgery-time, changing-time, wash-time, supervision and distribution of sweets and other extras, the whole day being punctuated with recognizable events through to bed-time. She regarded herself as an essential pivot for the running of the school, and she kept her distance from the masters, finding that on occasions they could be an unwholesome influence.

The new boys at the beginning of term had a different reception. Their parents were asked to drive round to the front door, and the Headmaster and his wife were there to welcome them. They were invited into the hall, and some parents, reluctant to part from their young one, might be entertained in the drawing-room, until the bedtime routine of the school compelled them to depart.

Millie was keenly interested in the new boys. They would be the ones nearest in age to herself, some of them barely two years older, and they would still be inexperienced and malleable. She might even find one to have as a friend, so an early inspection was important. She stationed herself on the landing half-way up the stairs in the hall. The stairs were to one side of the hall, so she was not too conspicuous, and the landing gave her a clear view of the front door. She leant against the bannisters, ready to wait the whole afternoon.

The first new boy to arrive was hardly new at all, as his older brother was already at the school. He grinned knowingly and was impatient to be away to the boys' quarters. Millie's father and mother greeted his parents with jokes and handshakes, and made remarks about the boy being called Brown Minor. His brother, who had been called plain Brown, would now be Brown Major. Millie dismissed Brown Minor as being too well up in the ways of the school to make a good friend.

The next boy was called Draper, she heard. He waited in the hall while his parents spoke at length to Millie's parents. His grey suit was obviously new, and too large, and his grey socks and black lace shoes were new, and his school tie was new, and he stood shaking with tears. He did not cry or open his mouth, but his whole body shook and tears streamed down his face. He looked round and saw Millie, and they stared glumly, neither being able to assist the other. Eventually Millie's mother spoke sweetly to Draper and held out her hand, and she led him and his parents away through the green baize door to the boys' quarters. Millie noted Draper as a possible friend.

Her father was standing alone when the next new boy arrived, with what Millie took to be his father, and they were of spectacular interest, being the first coloured people Millie had seen at the school. The man was tall and dark-skinned and notably dressed in a white suit and a broad-brimmed black hat, which he took off with a flourish as he entered the hall. The boy had paler skin, hardly dark at all, but his hair was jet black, thick

68

and combed away from his face. He was not wearing the grey school uniform jacket, but a fashionable navy-blue blazer with gold buttons, and he walked in the hall with self-assurance, looking round and giving a dismissive nod to Millie, as she gazed with awe through the bannisters. Her father took them directly into the drawing-room, leaving the hall bleakly empty.

Millie needed information, and fast, so she nipped down the stairs, across the hall and through the green baize door into the long corridor. At once she met her mother, returning with Draper's parents but without Draper.

'Ah, Millie darling, say how do you do to Mrs. and Mrs. Draper, will you?' Then even more sweetly, 'this is my daughter Millicent. She lives with us at the school, you know, it gives such a homely atmosphere for the younger boys.'

'How do you do,' Millie said, looking at them politely, as this was not the occasion for making difficulties, poised as she was on one foot ready to continue her sprint down the corridor. The Draper parents smiled and nodded in a bemused way, and went bereft and bravely back through the green baize door.

Next Millie met Matron at the bottom of the school stairs, holding Draper by the hand. He was still shaking, and he did not attempt to hide his tear-drenched face. 'And this is Millie,' Matron said cheerfully. 'She will help to make you feel more at home, won't you Millie?' She swung Draper's arm. 'She is younger than you are, so you don't need to be afraid of her.' Draper and Millie summed each other up, which satisfied Matron. 'Millie, why don't you come with us while I show Draper his dormitory?'

'Can't now, I'm busy,' Millie said hurriedly, and shot off down the corridor. She came to the boys' library, which was used by the younger boys as a common room, and she timidly went in through the open door. The boys were very noisy inside, excited to see each other again, and a mock fight had broken out with some of the boys hitting each other over the heads with books. Brown, in his new position as Brown Major, shouted orders, and Brown Minor over-stepped his privileged start and shouted too.

All their efforts were louder than usual, as they established themselves, and they fought early to see who would come out top this term.

Wellington was jumping up and down near the door and giggling. He was small for his age, with strong spectacles and bright ideas. He had been new the previous term, and the other boys had repeatedly called him 'Boots', with variations, but he had giggled through it all and remained unperturbed.

'Hello Millie,' he said, laughing and watching the other boys.

Millie stood beside him and spoke up to be heard. 'How many new boys this term?'

'Matron says three.' The necessary information had been exchanged, and the conversation was over.

'Hello Millie,' Masseau called out. He was a pretty boy, everyone agreed, and his long wavy fair hair fell elegantly over one side of his face.

'Hello Millie', Spink called nervously. He had to work hard not to remain down-trodden.

Masseau had to assert himself. 'Silly Millie wears a Pinny,' he chanted, 'Boots Boots Wellington Boots.' But his bantering was lost in the general hubbub, and Millie decided it was time to leave.

Further down the corridor, there was almost as great a noise from the masters' common room. Deep raucous laughs came through the open door, and the witticisms were shouted loud and clear. Miss West, the gym mistress, was poised in the doorway, holding up her hand for silence. When she saw Millie in the corridor, she quickly jumped round, slipped her hands under Millie's arms from behind, and lifted her up in the air. She entered the common room and once inside she held her arms up, so that Millie's legs dangled in front of her face. Millie could feel Miss West's hands on her ribs, firm and confident, and the masters looked up at her, their mouths open as they smiled and called out their jokes. Miss West moved slowly from side to side, and Millie felt the puffs of breath on the backs of her knees as they swung across.

70

'Well who am I now?' Miss West shouted out with heavier breaths. 'Come on, who am I now?'

'You're Ruboff the Russian weight-lifter.'

'No, no, you're the Olympic torch bearer.'

Millie looked down at the grinning faces. The English master cupped his hands over his mouth and called out, 'you're the Virgin Mary,' and this was followed by loud guffaws. Millie received extra shakes while Miss West laughed as she jogged.

'I know,' called out the aging games master, 'I know. You're Bovis winning the World Cup.'

'Right,' Miss West shouted triumphantly, and she gave Millie a final big swing as she slid her to the ground so that Millie's feet kicked up and her dress fell back, revealing her white knickers. Then she stood Millie in front of her and placed her hands on Millie's shoulders, smiling proudly at the audience. All the masters applauded, and Miss West held her arms out wide and bowed. Millie turned to go and Miss West quickly leant down and gave her a rough smacking kiss on the cheek, while the laughter and clapping went on. Millie left to cries of 'Encore' from the masters and Miss West's gurgly laugh above them all.

Hamble, Millie thought, knew all the answers, as she ran back up the corridor, rejecting every door on each side until she reached the pantry. There Hamble was, bustling and busy, turning from the cupboards to the tray on the table, preparing tea for the drawing-room. His shirt sleeves were glistening white, blossoming out from his tight black waistcoat, and, with his white apron tied round his black trousers, he flashed like a beacon as he moved around.

'Aha, my Missie Millie.' He stopped for a moment and smiled. 'Sit you down, then I won't be tripping over you.' He pulled out a chair at the table. 'Here's a cream biscuit to keep you going.' He put an extra plate down on the table, dropped a biscuit onto it, and leant over confidentially. 'Have you seen our Prince?'

Millie sat down with a sigh of relief. She could rely on Hamble to unravel the mystery. 'The black man that came is a Prince?' she said.

'Oho, no. It's the boy.' Hamble almost whispered. 'He's a Crown Prince. And he's coming to this school.'

'Crown?' Millie remembered the hatless boy. 'What's a Crown Prince?'

'It means,' Hamble said importantly, 'that he will be King one day.'

Millie was very impressed. 'So the black man is a King?'

'Ah, not so lucky.' Hamble laughed. 'Prince Fezel, for that is how we are to call the boy, came with his uncle. His father, the King,' Hamble whispered again, 'is much too busy to come here with the Prince.' Hamble spun round to the cupboard and flexed his arms. 'And I'm a busy man too, eh?' He quickly went on loading the tray. 'Kings, princes, you, me, we're all human, aren't we?' he added with finality.

'Can I have tea in the drawing-room?' Millie asked.

'Ah, not today.' Hamble whispered, as he did whenever the subject was impressive. 'They are discussing very important business.'

Suddenly, and uncharacteristically, her mother appeared in the doorway. 'Millie darling.' She sounded surprised. 'How lucky to find you.' She smiled deferentially at Hamble. 'We're ready for tea, Hamble, whenever you are.' Then she spoke hardly less deferentially to Millie. 'Darling, would you like to show Prince Fezel the gallery room? Just for a tiny time, while we talk over some things?' She smiled uncertainly. 'I'm sure he's longing to meet you.'

Millie slowly got down off her chair, and her mother continued her encouragement. 'It will only be for a minute, so he's not alone.' Her hand fluttered vaguely. 'We've got some important business to discuss.' She smiled as she left the pantry. 'Will you come now, darling?'

Millie turned to Hamble and they both grinned knowingly, then Hamble leant forward and whispered, 'you'll be a princess yet,' and Millie ran after her mother.

Through the green baize door again, she joined her mother and Fezel as they crossed to the far side of the hall. Her mother turned at the door to the gallery room.

'There you are, dears. We won't be long.' She opened the door and waved her arm in a vague flourish. 'Darling, do show the Prince round.' She smiled more elegantly than usual and left them.

Millie went in and looked down the little-used room. There was not much to say about it. Down one side there were tall windows looking out on the shrubbery at the side of the house, and the other side of the room was entirely filled with books, both below the narrow gallery and above, right up to the moulded ceiling. At one end there was a small spiral staircase leading to the gallery, but Millie suspected the whole structure as being unnatural and unsafe, and she had never seen anyone use it. The books were in heavy shelves fronted by latticed doors, as if they had to be prevented from leaping out. This added to the ominous oppression of the room.

'This is the gallery-room,' Millie said, without enthusiasm. Surely for the Prince there should be silk cushions and peacock-feather fans and golden goblets? Fezel walked in and looked around, and he seemed amused.

'Is that a very old picture?' He pointed to a long photograph, hung on the wall between the windows, showing the school in the early days, with stern masters sitting in a row on chairs and boys in their stiff white collars sitting cross-legged in front and standing in ranks behind.

Millie peered up at it. 'That's one of the first school photos. They haven't got the same uniform now.' There were other photographs hung between the windows, showing the football team with boys in striped shirts, and the cricket team with boys in caps and jackets. Millie knew them all, and she found them austere and gloomy. In the later ones she could hardly recognize her father, sitting in the middle with his arms crossed and a sick expression on his face. But they seemed to interest Fezel.

'This is last year's,' Millie said, pointing to one at the end of the room. 'It's got all the boys in it. They had to stand very still for ages.'

73

But Fezel had stopped at the team photographs. 'I know how to play cricket,' he said brightly. 'We formed a team with my uncles at home.' He looked at the football team. 'But my father is very keen that I should learn how to play football. He says that is just as important.'

'Football is easy,' Millie said, thinking of the boys rushing wildly backwards and forwards across the field. 'But you won't play football in the summer term.'

'I know.' Fezel looked at Millie for the first time and smiled. 'But I can score lots of runs at cricket, can't I?' They both giggled and wandered together across the room. Fezel peered between the criss-cross wooden lattices in front of the books and poked his finger at the gold titles.

'These aren't very interesting books,' he said with disgust. 'Are there any with coloured pictures?'

'I've got much more interesting books in my room,' Millie said proudly. 'I'll show them to you.'

'All right.' Fezel immediately stood to attention beside her, waiting for her to lead the way. Millie was taken aback by the speed of his decision, but since this must be the way that sons of kings behaved, she obediently turned and went out of the gallery room, up the stairs, along the landing and up to her multi-purpose room. She opened the door carefully, hoping that Miss Ellen would not be there, but happily the room was empty and she could lead Fezel confidently to her small bookcase.

'These books have got pictures in,' she said. She had been given some Children's Classics, and she had poured over the illustrations, piecing together the story. She pulled out 'Treasure Island' and opened it at the frontispiece. 'This one is exciting.'

Fezel looked over her shoulder. 'I know that one,' he said. 'Have you got any about horses?' He looked along the other books. 'My father keeps lots of horses, and I love stories about them.'

Millie thought hard about the other pictures. 'I think this one has got a horse in it.' She pulled out a tall book and put it flat on the table, turning the pages until she found a picture of a horse galloping, its mane flying in the wind, with its rider holding aloft a thin sword, his cloak billowing round him and the huge feather in his hat flying about. He was followed by two more galloping horses, with the riders waving their swords, and in front there were men behind a rock, levelling guns at them.

'That's a good one,' Fezel said excitedly, then he slowly read out the caption beneath the picture. 'It's an ambush, cried Dartagnon, ride on.' He smiled at Millie. 'Do you know what it's about?'

'They have adventures,' Millie said, pointing to the men on horseback. Fezel turned the pages, stopping to look at the pictures of men fighting with swords, men fighting with their fists, men holding up mugs and shouting, men galloping down dark streets, and finally a colourful picture of a huge ballroom with men and women in magnificent clothes. Millie pointed to a large man in the centre of the picture with particularly splendid lace collar and cuffs and glittering pendants and rings.

'That's the king,' she said. 'Is that what your father is like?'

Fezel shrieked with glee, staggered back and did a mock fall. He lay on his back and kicked his legs like a puppy, and rolled from side to side. 'Hoo hoo hoo, hoo hoo hoo,' he laughed, and Millie watched with delight. Then he leapt up agilely.

'I am going to have my own horse,' he said, suddenly serious. 'I shall choose a black one, and a good jumper. And I will have real leather cowboy boots, and a hat with an enormous brim.' He held his hands out wide each side of his head. 'And a belt.' He put his hands on his hips. 'Have you any books about cowboys?'

'No,' Millie said, crestfallen.

'They are the best riders of all. They can ride bare-back on an unbroken horse. Did you know that?'

'No,' Millie said sadly.

'They catch steers with their lassoes. Do you know what a steer is?'

'No,' Millie said, becoming grumpy.

'It's a young bull. I can make a lasso, I'll show you. Have you any rope?'

'I've got some string,' Millie said firmly, and she went to her drawer where she kept her collection of bits and pieces, hidden under a drawing book to protect it from prying eyes, and she pulled out a long piece of thick rough string.

'I can't make a lasso with that,' Fezel said doubtfully.

'It's the thickest piece I've got,' Millie said, and she handed it to him.

'I'll try,' he said. 'Take this end.' Millie held on tightly to one end of the string and watched intently. 'First you make a loop here, then you take the other end and you put it through here, and round here, twice, and back through here and then pull it tight.' He pulled at the bulky knot, and Millie let go of her end, so that he could swing the string loop in a wide circle above his head. 'Like that,' he said triumphantly. 'Now you've got to catch something.' He looked round and picked on a teddy bear on top of the chest of drawers, and he placed the string over the bear's head. 'If it was a proper rope, I could swing it round and catch the bear.' He pulled the loop tight. 'And then as the bear struggles, the lasso tightens and he can't get away.' He picked up the string and swung the bear round and round in circles above his head, letting out shouts and whoops, while Millie jumped and laughed and held up her hands towards the bear. They both ran round the room, shouting and hallooing, and Fezel swung the bear against the walls and cupboards, knocking down some of the pinned-up letter cards. They were making such an engrossing noise that they did not hear the door open.

'What are you doing?' Millie's mother stood inside the room, watching with amazement. She seemed more amused than angry, but her arms fluttered with alarm. 'You must stop that now, do stop it.'

Fezel and Millie stood still at once, like a game of grandmother's footsteps, and watched warily. They were slightly out of breath, and Fezel coughed and pulled out his handkerchief.

'You mustn't be so rough,' Millie's mother said plaintively. 'Millie darling, we must take care of Prince Fezel, he's a little bit delicate, his chest is not so strong.'

Millie looked with curiosity at Fezel, who dropped the bear and put away his handkerchief. 'I'm all right, Mrs. Newman,' he said in a commanding tone. 'We were only playing.'

'If you say so,' she said, relieved. 'That's all we've got time for now, dears. Will you come down and say goodbye to your uncle?' She held out her hand nervously towards Fezel. 'We've finished our little talk.'

'All right,' Fezel said, and stood sharply to attention.

Millie's mother looked round distractedly. 'Millie, you may as well stay here, it's nearly your suppertime.'

Millie watched them go with real sorrow. It had turned out to be one of her best afternoons, and she must find a way of playing with Fezel again. A lasso might come in useful, and she would look out for a piece of good rope. Meanwhile, she took the string and studied the lasso knot very carefully, and then practised her own knots at the other end of the string, until her supper arrived.

6

The school work of the boys was frequently a puzzle to Millie. In fact sometimes it was so mysterious that she thought a complete secret language must be being taught. The signs of the language were thick lines, crossing each other, with ordinary letters at each end, and triangles with a letter at each corner, and then circles with triangles inside and more letters and lines.

'Geometry,' her father had said briefly, when Millie asked him what all the lines and shapes were called. Either the language told of secrets so important that Millie had no inkling of them, or it was completely useless. Millie suspected it was the latter, but she kept her options open to please her father.

Ever since the Easter holiday, she had been allowed on occasions to visit her father's study. She did not know if this was connected with her Subsiduary Rehearsal, but she guessed it was because she found her father was giving her much more attention, watching her at meal times, taking her for short walks on Sunday afternoons, occasionally reading her a chapter from 'Alice in Wonderland' before she went to bed, and then, on some quiet afternoons, asking her to come to his study while he corrected the boys' work books.

Millie knelt on a chair at the side of the large flat-topped desk, with paper and pencil in front of her. The desk had inlaid green leather, to indicate its importance, and Millie discovered the principle of rubbings by placing her paper over the patterned edge of the leather and scribbling with her pencil to bring out the pattern on the paper. But her father did not like that when he noticed what she was doing, and she then started copying the lines and circles and letters from the work books.

Her father had covered the desk with the boys' books. There

was a pile of open books in front of him, and piles of closed books on each side. He would scrutinize the open book, add some marks with his pen, and then place the book on the closed pile. He taught mathematics, his one subject, throughout the school, and he had accumulated a lot of books for correction.

'What are you writing?' Millie asked, when she noticed that the marks he made were not letters.

'If the results of the exercises are correct, I mark them with a tick, and if the results are incorrect, I mark them with a cross.' He derived considerably pleasure from his activity.

Millie practised ticks and crosses on her piece of paper. She wanted to put crosses by the open lines because she found these most unsatisfactory and she had a great urge to join up the ends, in spite of the letters attached to each end. The triangles and circles were much pleasanter shapes and merited ticks. But on peering over the work books she found no rhyme or reason for the ticks and crosses. It could all be a great ruse to keep her father happy. She watched him pause, then make a tick, then pause, and then make a cross. It did not look very difficult.

'Can I do the ticks for you?' Millie asked eventually.

He leant back in his swivel chair. 'So you wish to become an assistant mathematics teacher?' His head tilted to one side and the corners of his mouth went down, so she knew that he was joking.

'I can do ticks. Look.' She held up her paper showing ticks of all sizes, and he looked at them with his head tilted and his mouth down.

'Very well then. I can see your ticks are up to standard.' He pulled the next work book towards him. 'When I am ready, you mark the book with a tick exactly where I show you.'

Millie eagerly moved her chair next to his, climbed up and leant across the desk, holding her pencil poised ready for action. It seemed a long wait while he stared at the book, and then he pointed to a space in the squared paper. 'A tick there,' he said briskly, and Millie carefully drew a neat tick. 'You must be quicker next time,' he said, already impatient, and she took this as permission to make untidy ticks in future.

He turned the page, frowned, grunted, and made two crosses at the side of the paper. She had to wait for the next work book for her second tick, which she did with a flourish. Already she was finding that the stretches of inactivity were hardly justified by the brief excitement of action. However, the realization of the honour of her position kept her going.

'Whose book is that?' she asked, when he pulled the next one down towards him.

'Wellington, I believe,' he said, looking at the name on the front cover. 'Yes, Wellington. His book is always neat.' She was pleased to be able to give him three successive ticks.

'Have we done Fezel's book?' she asked casually.

'Ah, yes, Fezel,' he said in a heavy tone. 'Fezel hands in his book when he feels like it. Fezel thinks he knows better than his teachers. Fezel considers he is somebody special.' He slapped his hand on the top of the desk. 'Fezel needs a good talking to.'

Millie was surprised at her father's vehemence, and she thought long and hard while waiting for her next tick.

'The new boys need a homely atmosphere,' she eventually said, in a grand voice.

'What?' her father said sharply.

'That's what my mother said,' she added crisply.

'Your mother doesn't always know what she's talking about,' he said crossly, and then he quickly tried to mollify the statement. 'That is to say, the school discipline requires a toughening process, which your mother does not fully appreciate. She takes a softer outlook with the young boys,' he grunted and absent-mindedly turned a page. 'Which I dare say has its place,' he added bitterly, and firmly marked a tick on the page.

'I do the ticks,' Millie cried out.

Her father's head tilted. 'So you are a keen new assistant.' He pointed to the next page, and Millie gave a flamboyant tick.

'Can I have some boys to tea for my birthday?' she said mildly. Her birthday always fell at the beginning of the summer term, and it had been a dull affair the previous year, with a brief tea with her parents. 'We could have tea in my room, and then we could play games.'

'What boys had you in mind?' her father said, surprised.

'Just one or two of the younger boys,' she said in her casual tone.

He pointed to the page for a tick. 'No doubt an exception could be made for this occasion.' He paused again to mark a cross. 'It would have to be on a Sunday, and even then they would miss Sunday assembly.'

'I'm sure they wouldn't mind that,' she said eagerly.

He leant back. 'I have no doubt that they would relish the opportunity to be absent from the Sunday divinity talk.' He looked quite fierce, and his head was not tilted. 'I have noticed an unfortunate tendency among the younger boys to treat the moral lecture with less than its proper seriousness.'

Millie waited while silent respect was given to moral talks. After another tick, she said, 'can I ask some boys, then?'

He sighed and put down his pen. 'Let me see, when is your birthday.' He opened the drawer of his desk and pulled out a calendar.

'It's on Friday, I know, I looked it up with Miss Ellen,' she said quickly.

'Friday week,' he said. 'That's right.' He stared at the calendar as if for guidance. 'The following Sunday, then,' he said gruffly. 'You may ask some boys to tea. But they must be back for prep hour.'

'Couldn't they miss that as well?' she said, trying her luck.

'No, no,' he said firmly. 'They write their letters home then.' His head tilted slightly. 'You must not interfere with their missives to their parents.' He leant forward to finish the last few books.

'I'll ask them tomorrow,' she said quietly, 'in afternoon break-time.' She was losing interest in the infrequent ticks, and she looked round for something else to do. The study was a small room, particularly for a headmaster, but her father had chosen it for its convenient situation next to the masters' common room and opposite the prefects' room. It was filled with papers, in filing cabinets and on the bookshelves and in neat piles on another large table and on the mantelpiece. The small fireplace had been another attaction in the room for her father, as he liked the cheerfulness of a coal fire in the winter, and even now, in the summer term, there were ashes in the grate from a recent fire. Millie got down from her chair, took her piece of paper and put it in the grate. This was a good chance to practise lighting matches, but even after a thorough search she could not find a box. Her father had cleared away the mathematics books and he was furiously filling in report forms, so she hesitated to interrupt him. Instead, she collected another piece of paper and her pencil and she sat back in the large black leather armchair beside the fireplace. The chair was a favourite of her father's, and it had shiny grease marks on the arms and back. Millie's head came well below the shiny marks, and her feet, stretched out before her, only just reached the front edge of the chair. She rested her paper on her knees and thought about writing a list of the boys she would invite. Such a list would be important and influential, and she must write it carefully. Furthermore, she must try to write it all on her own, to keep the list untainted by outside influence, which might reduce its power. It was for just such an occasion that she had been spending her effort on learning to write.

The first name that came to mind was Wellington. He would surely be good at thinking up games. She wrote 'w' neatly at the top of the paper, and then next to it 'e' and then 'l', and then she stopped. Spelling was such an inpenetrable struggle, but she must find a way or the list would be useless. Finally she added 'n' 't' 'u' 'n', and regarded the satisfactory result, 'welntun'.

Of course she must ask Fezel, and she wrote without hesitation 'f' 'e' 's' 'l', underneath the first name, as was proper for a list. Then she decided that Spink would be useful as he would do as he was told, so she wrote 's' 'p' 'i', and then, remembering a configuration from a recent lesson, she added 'n' 'g', and afterwards 'c'. Then she remembered about 'k'.

'How do I do a 'k'?' she asked, breaking the silence of concentration.

Her father twisted his head round to look at her over his shoulder. 'The letter 'k' consists of a vertical line with two shorter oblique lines placed to the right in opposing directions.' The corners of his mouth went down and he shuffled his legs. Millie looked at him steadily, and it dawned on her that jokes could become an appalling nuisance.

She studied her paper again and left the name as it stood, 'spingc'. She thought of the new boy Draper and his tears, and she wrote 'd' 'r' 'a' 'e' 'p' 'e'. Then Masseau could be fun, and there was the other new boy Brown Minor, so she added 'm' 'a' 's' 'o', and 'b' 'r' 'o' 'w' 'n' was a word she knew, and then 'm' 'y' because Minor was always abbreviated. These were all the boys who came first to mind and whom she knew best, and any more might be difficult to handle.

She looked at the names down the paper.

'welntun'

'fesl'

'spingc'

'draepe'

'maso'

'brown my'

It was a true list, palpitating with magic, and she savoured it with intense pleasure.

'What have you got there?' Her father stood up, head tilted, and put his hands in his trouser pockets. 'You have been working hard all this time. Is it a letter to your parent?' He proudly jingled the loose money in his pocket.

Millie at once folded the paper. She was alarmed that critical eyes would evaporate the magic. 'I was practising my letters,' she said coolly.

'Do you know your alphabet as well as your ticks?' Jingling, he came to the side of the chair, his whole stance emanating satisfaction.

'I'll write out the alphabet specially for you,' she said, folding the paper again and again, and, with difficulty, again, until she had a hard wedge of paper, held tightly in her hand.

'Is this one not good enough for me?' He sounded piqued. 'Let me see how you are progressing.'

She looked up at him, and said slowly and sweetly, 'I would like to do a neat one for you'.

'Most commendable,' he said, oozing satisfaction again. 'I see you have the right attitude.' He returned to his desk and started gathering up his papers. 'I expect to see a neatly-executed alphabet tomorrow.'

She wriggled down off the chair. 'I'll go and do it now,' she said confidently. 'Then you can have it at bedtime, if you come and read to me.' They both heard the burst of distant cries as the boys came in to the changing-room from afternoon games.

'Hurry along now,' he said, suddenly agitated. 'Time is moving on.' He opened his side drawer where he kept his diary and glanced at the day's appointments. 'I will be up later to read to you, but for a short time only this evening.'

'I could read to you,' she said, with a sudden urge to show off. 'I can read quite well now.'

'We will do that on another afternoon.' He was concentrating on stacking the papers, moving the books, searching out files and looking up letters.

'Next time I come here,' she said, to make it quite clear, 'I will bring my book and I will read it to you.' Before her father could reply, there was a loud knock on the door.

'Come in,' he called out, and Miss West bounded in, flushed from exercise and still in her gym shirt and shorts, with a heavy whistle hung round her neck.

'Henry, only you can help me,' she said breathlessly. 'That young devil Fezel is impossible, I can't control him.' She had not seen Millie, standing at the far side of the room beyond the desk.

'Yes.' Her father paused indecisively, holding a letter in his hand, then he flapped the letter up and down. 'Come in, Miss West, come in. We can discuss the matter.' He pushed a pile of letters across his desk. 'Millie, it is time for you to go now.'

'Oh, Millie,' Miss West cried out. 'I didn't see you there. How are you doing?' She rushed over and squatted in front of Millie, bringing her untidy and sweaty hair to the level of Millie's nose. 'You must come down to the gym one day, when there's just the two of us, and I'll show you the wall bars and the ropes. You can learn to climb a rope, that would be fun.'

Millie brightened at this idea. 'I would like to do that,' she said politely.

'You will be having a busy time, Millie,' her father said heartily. 'Now you must return to your room.' He looked at his watch. 'I believe it will soon be your suppertime.'

'Not yet,' Millie said crossly, but she slowly went towards the door.

Miss West flopped down into the leather armchair, leaning back and looking very much at home. 'Bye, Millie,' she said, with a smile and a tired wave of her hand. 'I'll arrange a day for you to come to the gym. Maybe tomorrow,' she added, smiling at Millie's father.

'We will see, we will see,' he said, sitting at his desk and frowning at the letters.

'Goodbye,' Millie said at the door, and both the adults replied, 'goodbye, goodbye.' She left them poised in inactivity, waiting for the final moment of her departure. She paused outside the closed door, but all she could hear was the noise from the boys in the changing room, and the corridor remained empty. So in the absence of anything more constructive making its appearance, she ambled towards the green baize door and her room beyond, still clutching the wedge of paper with the magic list intact.

7

The remains of a sumptuous tea were spread across the table in Millie's room. Cook had done her proud and provided her with a tea fit many times over for the birthday party of a Headmaster's daughter. The previous day, being a Saturday and no lessons, Millie had wandered through the kitchen, and Cook had spoken to her about the tea, asking what flavours she wanted for the jellies and cake. It was not usual for Cook to interest herself in Millie's tea, and Millie had suspected the kind help of Miss Case. Nonetheless it was Cook who had baked and iced the cake, and written 'Happy Birthday to Millie' in pink icing on top, and Millie was wildly delighted. To have won round Cook was a notable achievement.

Millie and the boys had ravaged their way through the sandwiches with four different fillings, the biscuits and buns, the cold sausages and the jellies, and finally the cake. Millie had wanted candles on the cake for the party, but her mother had protested. Candles were only to be on the smaller sponge cake for tea on the Friday of the birthday itself, held sedately in the drawing-room. Millie's father had not been able to be present, so her mother had at the last minute invited the two most senior masters available, in an attempt to make the occasion more festive. So it had been a strange tea, with Mr. Merryman, the games master, and Mr. Ambrose, the music master, making polite and inappropriate childish talk. Millie had pointed out that she was now six, with six candles on her cake, but to the masters this was an age younger than any they had to deal with in the school, and they were not able to graduate their talk between remarks appropriate for school boys and remarks addressed to little children. So Millie had blown out her candles, with one breath as urged by the masters, and she had silently wished for the extermination of all adults at the school. The masters had said that her wish would come true, and she had thrown in all the other adults to be on the safe side. Better safe than sorry, as Miss Ellen would say, which was another reason for throwing her in as well. Millie had smiled sadly and unrelentingly at her mother, realizing that sacrifices must be made before the grand sweep of her wish, and she contemplated the world with only herself and the boys in it.

The boys had not objected to the absence of candles on the cake in Millie's room. The icing on the cake was good enough, and indeed the presence of the cake itself, or even the fact that they were there at all, was cause for keen excitement among the boys. They had been selected, for whatever reason, as being beyond the needs of the Sunday moral indoctrination, and even if they missed only one Sunday assembly, it rendered them morally superior and gave them licence for their own standards of behaviour. Certainly their table manners had been affected, and they had leant over the table, eating a bit of this and a bit of that, stuffing in more food and laughing gleefully with their mouths full. They had been prevented from actually throwing the food by the inhibiting presence of Miss Ellen in one corner of the room.

Throughout the tea, Miss Ellen had sat in front of the cupboard door beside the fireplace, her feet on a small stool and her head bowed over her knitting. The whole event was so novel that no one had known whether Miss Ellen should remain in the room, or whether the tea party could be safely left unattended. In the end, after discussions in the drawing-room, Miss Ellen herself had decided to stay, to satisfy herself that no damage was done either by or to her charge. But she could not call out admonishments because there were no rules laid down for such an event, so she sat silent, waiting only to curb extreme excesses.

It had been Miss Ellen's fault, Millie knew, that there were only three boys at the tea party, and it had made Millie aware of the communications system. She had told Miss Ellen straight

87

away about the tea, as soon as she had obtained her father's permission, and she had announced that there would be six boys, because after all she had to make sure that there would be enough food provided although she kept the list itself a guarded secret. But next day, even before she had had time to speak to the boys, Miss Ellen had told her that she could only have three boys, on the Headmaster's orders, and although Millie had argued hotly, almost tearfully, Miss Ellen had remained firm.

Millie realized that the selection of the boys was a great responsibility, and she had given it long consideration before going down to the boys' library at breaktime. She had chosen Wellington, Fezel and Draper, but when all the boys had discovered what was afoot and had crowded round her, she had not been able to resist telling the unsuccessful boys on the list that she would have invited them had she been allowed to, and this made her even more clamorously in demand. She was forced to copy Miss Ellen's firmness to protect herself from the noisy and pressing pleas.

By the time the three chosen boys had eaten up most of the cake, Millie was not so sure that she had made a wise selection. They did seem to be extra silly, and they were egging each other on. Fezel had lost many of his princely airs, and he had picked up in turn the habits of common schoolboys. Millie had been relying on him to augment her authority, and he had become considerably less attractive.

Wellington, on the contrary, was bossier than she had seen him, shouting out orders and then giving a shrieking giggle after each one. He was not always obeyed, but his giggle was infectious. Draper, now that his tears had gone, had turned out to be a wily boy, waiting and watching with a self-effacing smile until the moment was advantageous for him to bound in, and then he shouted and waved his arms like a tornado.

'Let's play some games,' Millie said, trying to keep a modicum of control over the party. The tea itself had deteriorated, with crumbs everywhere and unwanted spoonfuls of jelly splashed across the tablecloth.

'What games do we know?' Wellington said, and he immediately added, 'I know, we could play blind man's buff, and you,' he pointed at Millie and giggled, 'can be the blind man.'

Millie scowled, but Fezel spoke first. 'What is a buff? I do not know this game.' He had somewhat regained his princely grand manner. 'Does it require a team?'

'Or better still,' Wellington said, bubbling with suggestions, 'we could play musical chairs, we could go round the table, and I'll take a chair away.' He kicked at the legs of his chair.

'I do not know this game either,' Fezel said indignantly. 'Does it require music?'

'I can play the recorder,' Draper shouted, waving his fingers in front of his mouth. 'I could go round the table playing the recorder, and then when I stop we all sit down.'

'That won't work,' Millie shouted at him crossly. 'You would know before us when you were going to stop, and then you would sit down first.'

'Sardines,' Wellington shouted. 'Sardines. Let's play sardines.' Millie looked round the room for hiding places, and saw Miss Ellen frowning over her knitting in front of the best place of all, the capacious cupboard.

Wellington did not wait for Fezel's objections and he started explaining at once. 'One person hides, and the others count up to twenty, no, better still, fifty, and then they start looking and when one finds him he hides with him as well until there is only one left and he's the one who's lost.'

Fezel listened carefully. 'That's not a bad game. But there aren't enough of us.' He also looked round. 'And the room isn't big enough. Can we play outside?'

Miss Ellen spoke for the first time. 'You have to stay in the room,' she said loudly and clearly, without looking up from her knitting, and there was a crest-fallen silence.

'Let's just play Cowboys and Indians,' Draper said, standing up and pointing the fingers of both hands as imitation pistols. 'Pow. Pow. Two of us can be cowboys, and the other two Indians.'

'Fezel knows all about cowboys,' Millie said excitedly. 'He can be one of the cowboys with a lasso.'

'All right,' Fezel said graciously. 'And I'll choose Millie to be on my side.' He had learnt diplomacy early in his life.

'But I wanted to be a cowboy,' Draper said plaintively, looking close to tears.

'Come on, Draper, don't be a sissy,' Wellington said cheerfully. 'We'll be the Indians and we'll plan a surprise attack.' He went to the corner where there was Millie's bed and chest of drawers, and he turned round and held his arms out wide. 'This is our camp. You can't come in here without a fight to the death.' He quickly and noisily dragged two chairs to the corner. 'Come on Draper. Help make a barrier.'

Millie suddenly ducked down and crawled under the table. 'This is our house,' she called out. The large tablecloth came half-way down the sides of the table, and she was remarkably well hidden.

'We must have some weapons,' Fezel said, standing in front of the table.

'They'll be in the cupboard.' Millie crawled out again and stood up. 'Please Miss Ellen, I want to get at my toys.' The bottom of the cupboard held a large open box where her toys were thrown unceremoniously. Her pieces which she valued more highly, though to others they appeared as bits and scraps, were kept in her own drawer by her bed, and she found she could even leave her magic list there untouched, so unimportant did it seem.

Miss Ellen stood up, hardly taking her eyes off her knitting, and she carried the knitting and the chair to the other corner by the window. Only then did she turn round and survey the wrecked remains of the tea. 'I will clear this away.' She sighed grimly. 'I don't want any breakages.'

Millie and Fezel were already leaning over the box, pushing the toys backwards and forwards and examining them as a potential armoury, and Wellington and Draper tried in vain to push in between them, wanting a good choice for the defence of their camp.

'You have bows and arrows anyway,' Millie said to them, from deep in the box. 'I've got a gun somewhere. Oh, look, here it is.' She held up a detailed replica of a pistol, all in solid silver plastic, and put her finger on the immovable trigger.

'That'll do,' Fezel said. 'I'll use this.' He picked up a wooden pop-gun with a cork in the end.

'Indians have rifles too,' Wellington said, trying to get hold of a drum stick at one end of the box.

'We could use those, up there, they would do for bows,' Draper shouted, pointing to the hangers holding Millie's dresses and jackets and coats at the top of the cupboard.

Millie spun round in alarm, looking for Miss Ellen. The plates were stacked in a pile on the table, the crumbs were brushed to one end, but Miss Ellen was not there.

'Quick, quick,' Millie said. She pulled the footstool to the cupboard and stood on it to reach her coat.

'I can reach without that,' Fezel said, and he tugged at the dresses. They both pulled down the clothes, letting them fall into the box, and Wellington picked up the tumbling hangers. Fezel threw down the remaining hangers, and they shared them out, two each and two left over.

'We should have the extra ones,' Wellington said, 'if they're meant to be bows. Have you any string?'

'Quick,' Millie said, still in the absence of Miss Ellen. She ran to her drawer and brought out her collected bits of string, and also the saved lasso which she handed to Fezel.

'Head-dresses,' she said. 'We must have hats.' She hurriedly rummaged through her chest of drawers and threw onto the floor a sou'wester, a woollen hat, belts, ribbons, a linen hat and a straw hat, adding to the offerings as she came to them, while the boys snatched them up and tried them on, marching round the table and calling out war cries. Wellington had tied a woollen scarf round his waist and pushed in the drum sticks. 'These are my arrows,' he shouted. 'And these,' he picked up a pink woollen glove and balanced it on his head, 'are my feathers.' Fezel had commandeered the straw hat and gave a succession of smart

91

salutes. Draper ran round, the black sou'wester tied with ribbons on his head, waving a belt as a whip and a coat hanger as an axe. 'Waaaoooowaaaoooowaaaoooo,' he called out. Millie tried pulling the woollen hat down over her ears and eyes, and carefully pointed her pistol. 'Bang,' she shouted. 'Bang. Bang.' 'Woowoowoowoo,' Wellington replied, banging his hand on his mouth.

Miss Ellen at last returned with Miss Case, both of them carrying empty trays. 'Quieter,' Miss Ellen called out sternly, and then, when the noise stopped, she added, 'I can hear you from half way down the stairs.' She stared straight ahead, hardly daring to inspect the extent of the disarray. 'All this must be cleared up afterwards,' she said, in a tired voice.

Miss Case waited behind, grinning at everyone, but she did not interfere with Miss Ellen's severe tone. They moved in on the table, wielding their trays, and Fezel stepped forward.

'Can I use that?' He tapped the tray. 'It would make a good shield.'

'Cowboys don't have shields,' Wellington said quickly.

Miss Case looked at them. 'So you are cowboys, are you?' she said, suppressing her laughter.

'He's an Indian,' Draper shouted, pointing at Wellington. 'And I'm an Indian.'

'Quiet,' Miss Ellen barked out. 'You must keep your voices down.' She paused to make sure that they obeyed. 'Let Miss Case carry on with her work.' The two women descended on the table, stacking the plates and the uneaten remains of food onto the trays.

Millie judged Miss Ellen's mood to be a good one, all things considered. Miss Ellen had hinted that their bounds were wide, and their game was acceptable, provided that the evidence of their activities remained unobtrusive, and for this they must stay in the room and shut up. Millie tried to convey this to the boys.

'Wellington, Draper,' she said in a half-whisper. 'You come behind your barricade.' She waved with her pistol at the row of

92

chairs in front of the bed. 'Then Fezel and I will go in our house, and then we can each plan to attack each other.' Her voice rose already with pleasurable anticipation.

'Sh,' Wellington said, catching on. 'We must keep our plans secret.'

'Can I have a pencil and paper?' Fezel said. 'I'll draw up a battle plan.' Millie fetched them for him at once from her bookcase, while Wellington and Draper busily gathered up all the available sticks and hangers and piled them behind the chairs.

'A torch would be useful,' Fezel said, as he stood waiting for the table to be cleared. 'Binoculars too, if you have any.'

'We must make our house comfortable,' Millie said, picking up her coat from the cupboard. 'We can use this to sit on.' She took a jacket as well, and cautiously carried them to where Fezel was standing in the middle of the room. But Miss Ellen paid no attention, concentrating on the nearly full tray.

'I know, I can be Fezel's wife,' Millie said brightly, and Wellington and Draper immediately giggled. Fezel looked down at the blank paper and pencil in his hand.

'You can't be a cowboy's wife,' Wellington sneered.

'Why not? I'm a girl,' Millie shouted indignantly.

'For now you're a cowboy, see,' Wellington yelled angrily, waving a hanger.

'Well I'll be a girl cowboy, see, and girls can be wives, so there.' Millie almost spat in her fury.

'There aren't girl cowboys,' Wellington shrieked. 'There aren't girl cowboys.'

'Well I'm going to be one.' Millie flung down her coat and jacket and stamped on them. 'I'm going to be a girl cowboy.'

'That's the spirit,' Miss Case said, and stood laughing so much that she was unable to lift her full tray.

Millie appealed to the arbiter, Miss Ellen. 'I can marry Fezel if I want to, can't I, if I'm a girl.'

But the whole scene was beyond Miss Ellen's capabilities of judgement, and she dismissed such profound problems for more practical matters. 'Hold the door open, will you?' she said grimly, unsteadily lifting her over-loaded tray.

Fezel went to the door and waited while Miss Ellen and Miss Case passed through. 'Have a good time,' Miss Case said to Fezel as she went by, grinning and nodding above her tray. 'You'll have to keep that unruly wife in order.' She laughed again from the corridor outside, and Fezel firmly shut the door behind her.

'Let's go on with the battle,' Fezel said grumpily.

'Are you going to be a cowboy, then?' Wellington said to Millie, a hint of triumph in his voice.

'You could be a squaw,' Draper shouted excitedly. 'Indians have wives, and if you were an Indian you could be a squaw.'

'Shut up, shut up,' Wellington and Fezel shouted together, and Wellington hit Draper with a hanger.

'Don't, don't,' Draper whined, holding up his arms to defend himself.

Millie picked up the coat and jacket and crawled under the table. 'It's quite comfortable here,' she called out. 'Come on.' Fezel dropped to his hands and knees and clutching paper, pencil and the pop-gun, he crawled forward, ducking under the tablecloth to prevent the straw hat being knocked off his head. Being taller than Millie, he could not sit up straight underneath the table, and while Millie sat erect, leaning against a table leg with her feet tucked neatly beneath her, he crouched uncomfortably with his legs sprawled in front of him and his black shoes knocking against her knees.

Millie felt strangely close to Fezel in the unexpectedly squashed confines under the table. She could hear whispers from Wellington and Draper, but the tablecloth cut off the view of the room except for the floor round the table. She felt more alone with him than ever before, and she was aware of his silence.

'I can marry you, can't I?' she whispered very quietly.

Fezel shuffled the paper in extreme embarrassment. 'You're not old enough,' he whispered back.

'But when I grow up,' she whispered, a warm confidence growing as he did not directly turn her down, 'then I can.'

Fezel gave her an odd sideways look. 'I don't think you know what being married means.'

'Yes I do,' Millie said crossly, becoming exasperated with the endlessly recurring insinuations. 'Of course I do. When we get married you'll see I do.'

'Are you ready?' Wellington called out. Millie put her head under the tablecloth and looked out at their preparations. They had turned the chairs upside-down and balanced the hangers on them to point towards the table, and Millie's teddy bear was tied horizontally between two chair legs.

'Our guns are ready to fire,' Draper cried, waving his hands at the hangers.

'What's the teddy bear?' Millie said, puzzled.

Wellington prodded it fiercely with the point of a pencil. 'This is our camp fire,' he said in a menacing voice. 'We're roasting the bear on a spit.' He slowly licked his lips and rubbed his hand over his stomach.

'We're not ready,' Fezel said loudly from behind the tablecloth. 'Come here Millie. I'll go through the plan.'

Millie returned to the cramped quarters under the table and knelt next to Fezel, who leant over and spoke in an urgent whisper. 'This is my plan.' He sternly shook the pencil at Millie. 'You crawl out at the front. Keep low, and move slowly, and this will draw their fire.' He paused. 'Got that?' Millie nodded unhappily. 'Then I will go out at the back, crawl round, and rush in with a surprise attack on their undefended flank.'

Millie frowned. 'Won't they see you coming?'

'That depends on you,' Fezel said firmly. 'It's your job to distract them.'

Millie sighed. 'I might get shot first.'

'No you won't,' Fezel said irritably. 'You guard yourself, shoot at them, do whatever you like, but you must keep their attention.'

Millie set her lips firmly, picked up her plastic pistol, and lay flat on her stomach. After a moment, she turned her head to Fezel and slowly mouthed under her breath, 'I'm going now.' Fezel nodded, and she started to inch forward.

'Aren't you ready yet?' Wellington called out crossly.

'Ready,' Fezel shouted, which made them all freeze still for an instant, in an unnatural silence. Then Fezel shifted impatiently, and kicked Millie hard in the shins to make her move forward again. She cautiously put her head out beyond the table, and then her hands, looking up to aim her pistol, but to her surprise the chairs were unattended and there was no sign of the enemy.

Suddenly Millie was hit violently on the head, making her jerk down and knock her forehead on the floor. Looking sideways she found her teddy bear beside her, and she realized that it had been thrown at her hard and accurately. Suddenly she was hit again by an even harder object, and then again, and her rabbit and her dormouse landed beside her. The enemy had found the drawer where her 'soft' toys were kept, and as she hunched her shoulders to defend herself she was aware of the two boys standing on the bed, determination on their faces, arms raised in readiness to throw further ammunition.

She bravely shuffled forward, and more objects hit her head and her back, softer this time, and she was surrounded by balls made out of rolled-up socks. There was still not a sign of Fezel, and Millie miserably wondered what object would come flying at her next. She was hit by two well-aimed paper darts, which she brushed away disdainfully, and then a pillow engulfed her head and knocked her to the floor again, which made her, for the first time during the party, intensely annoyed and dissatisfied.

She remained on the floor, covered by the pillow, as she found this was a useful defensive position, when screams and thuds and crashes broke out on both sides, and Millie bobbed up, fearful of what she would find. But it was, delightfully, the unfailing Fezel to the rescue. He had pushed through the barricade of chairs and he was standing on the edge of the bed, the tablecloth spread wide between his out-stretched arms, bearing down on Wellington and Draper who were pinned against the wall, screaming and kicking. Fezel pulled the tablecloth down over them, and they all fell on to the bed in a yelling, punching, struggling heap. Millie stood up and watched from the end of the

96

bed, half smiling and half alarmed, deeply envious, and she renewed yet more strongly her vow to overcome her handicap of being little and being a girl. Being naughty was all that was left to her, she concluded as she watched and waited.

Miss Ellen came in and stood gasping, staring in horror at the heaving pile of boys on the bed, until her anger overcame her. 'Off. Off. Off.' She yelled out the orders and Millie was impressed to see that the boys obeyed at once, wriggling off the bed and pulling their clothes straight as they stood up. They giggled as Wellington searched for his spectacles in the rumpled bedcover, which set off Miss Ellen again.

'Stop that nonsense,' she barked, and she glared steadily at them until they were all three standing in a row beside the bed. 'Now say you are sorry to Millie,' she ordered, and they all three turned their heads to where Millie was standing by the bottom of the bed.

'Sorry, sorry, sorry,' they muttered, and Wellington giggled uncontrollably when he caught Millie's eye. Millie received their apologies with amazement, finding herself in a wondrously regal position which she unhesitatingly accepted although she saw no reason for it.

'You have been privileged to come here for tea with Millie,' Miss Ellen went on, 'and then you make a mess of Millie's room.' Wellington still shook with silent giggles, but Fezel and Draper frowned crossly at her accusation.

'I want you to tidy up every single article before you leave,' she continued primly. 'Put everything back in its rightful place.'

'But Millie did it too,' Fezel burst out.

'That is beside the point.' Miss Ellen swept her hand wearily across her brow. 'You should be ashamed of yourselves, leading Millie on to such outrageous behaviour. However,' she added, raising her eyebrows and looking down at the boys. 'I have no doubt that Millie will help you tidy up.' She did not speak directly to Millie, but she looked round with disgust at the scattered relics of the battle. 'You can start with the socks,' she said, pointing to the floor, and then she saw the hangers. 'What's this? What's this?' Her voice squeaked with indignation, and she turned to the cupboard. Millie secretly kicked herself for leaving the door open, revealing the cupboard empty of clothes and hangers.

'Millie.' Miss Ellen was at her most authoritarian. 'Millie.' She stood squarely in the centre of the room, now looking straight at Millie. 'Where are your clothes?'

'In the box,' Millie stated directly. She knew that she would have to side, ultimately, with the boys, even if it meant losing Miss Ellen's support for her regality.

'Why are they in the box?' Miss Ellen made it sound rhetorical.

'So that we could take the hangers,' Millie chanted, as if it was another classroom lesson.

'Why did you take the hangers?' A note of curiosity crept in to Miss Ellen's voice.

'For bows,' Millie said.

'Bows?' Miss Ellen was astonished.

'Bows for the Indians,' Millie explained.

Miss Ellen looked at the discarded ribbons, still puzzled. 'For bows and arrows,' Draper said. The three boys were still standing in a row by the bed, and this drew Miss Ellen's attention to them.

'Hurry up, boys, hurry up. Get going.' The boys made a half-hearted effort to pick up the things nearest to them, and Fezel pulled at the bedcover to straighten it. 'Millie, you must be responsible for hanging up your clothes again.' But Miss Ellen did not leave it all to Millie. She went to the cupboard and picked the clothes out of the box, and as Millie brought her the hangers she shook the clothes out and hung them up. The boys had replaced the tablecloth and piled everything from the floor onto the table and put the chairs in position round the table. Now they rested against the backs of the chairs, waiting for approval.

'Well done, boys, well done,' Miss Ellen duly said, relieved that the party had not ended in a greater disaster. 'Is it time for you to go now?' she added hopefully.

Fezel looked at his large silver wrist-watch. 'We've still got a quarter of an hour,' he said cheerfully.

'Find something quiet to do,' Miss Ellen said vaguely, as she returned to her chair with the knitting.

'But what can we do that's quiet?' Millie said to her defiantly.

'You must be able to think of something,' Miss Ellen said, already buried in her knitting. 'You could let Fezel read to you.'

'Fezel read to us,' Wellington shrieked, doubling up with laughter.

'I could play a tune,' Draper shouted, jumping up and down. 'I could play on the recorder.'

'I know a good game,' Fezel said with dignity. 'Fetch me some stones.' There were no stones in the room, but they searched in the boxes on the bookshelf and collected some dice and counters, and Fezel knelt on the floor, spreading them out in front of him.

'This is how you play,' he said, picking up a dice.

'Oh, I know that game,' Draper said contemptuously, looking down at Fezel as he threw up the dice. 'It's called jacks.'

'Is that right?' Fezel said, looking up at Wellington who was standing with the others round Fezel.

'We have that game here,' Wellington stated without enthusiasm. 'I know,' he said helpfully. 'Why don't we play marbles? I saw some in the box.' They all fell gratefully on the marbles and spread themselves on the floor, contentedly rolling the glass balls until Miss Ellen finally pointed out the time.

'Say thank you to Millie,' Miss Ellen said, when the three boys were standing by the door, and they gave weak smiles and muttered. Millie smiled happily, feeling securely restored to her throne once more.

'Thank you very much for coming,' she said clearly. 'You can come again.' She waved goodbye as they left, and when Miss Ellen asked her to put away her things, she refused. She felt full of powerful satisfaction, knowing that the combination of herself and the boys had scared Miss Ellen, and she sensed that great possibilities were within her grasp. She had found her allies, and she would work on it for the term's project.

8

A message came through to Millie that some of the boys wanted to see her on Wednesday afternoon between games and supper. The message arrived in a strange way, through Nancy Matters. Nancy had come in one morning during Millie's lessons, with a piece of paper, and she told Millie that the boys had given it to Matron, and Matron had passed it on to her. 'It's an invitation,' Nancy said. 'You are to be downstairs,' she went on, looking again at the piece of paper. 'Outside the Junior Library, after changing time on Wednesday next.'

'Who's it from?' Millie asked.

Nancy peered at the signatures, and Miss Ellen took the paper from her. 'It's signed "Wilcox" and "Ash,"' Miss Ellen said to Millie. 'Do you know them?'

Millie frowned suspiciously. 'They're senior boys.'

Miss Ellen read out the message. 'To Millie Newman. You are kindly requested to attend a meeting of great importance when you will meet a person of great interest to you. This is an invitation you will not regret. Be outside the Junior Library,' Miss Ellen looked up, 'and so on. You may as well go, you never know, they might have prepared an entertainment for you.'

But Millie continued to be suspicious, and after lunch she slipped down to the library to see what she could find out. At first she could not find anyone she knew well, and she was forced to approach Collins, a serious boy who scorned girls more than most.

'Do you know anything about my meeting on Wednesday?' Millie asked him diffidently.

'Meeting? What meeting?' Collins sounded furious. Then he shrugged his shoulders and blew out his breath contemptuously.

'Pooh. I did hear something about it. You must ask Brown Mi, he knows more about that sort of thing.'

Some more boys came in, among them Spink, and Millie went over to him. 'Do you know about my invitation?' she said, pleased to see a younger boy.

'Your invitation?' Spink said, looking vaguely at his shoes. 'A bit. Someone will meet you outside the library on Wednesday.'

'I know that,' Millie said impatiently. 'Do you know any more about it?'

'No, no, it's nothing to do with me,' Spink said uncomfortably, and he moved away with the other boys. Millie was not reassured, and she waited in the hope that one of her appointed allies would arrive. Other boys arrived in twos and threes, and eventually Masseau came up to Millie.

'Can you come on Wednesday?' he said cheerfully. 'We've got everything arranged. There'll be someone to take you there.'

'Take me where?' Millie said, alarmed.

Massau laughed. 'Don't worry. There'll be someone with you all the time. You'll be all right.' He smiled and shook back his fair hair, and Millie had to be content with this. No one else arrived to give her a fuller explanation, so she had to assume that she would be in safe hands. She wandered back through the green baize door, unable to even guess what the boys could have in store for her.

On Wednesday Millie went down to the school corridor as soon as she heard the boys come in from games, and she waited obediently outside the library. Boys sauntered up from the changing room, laughing and chatting, but none of them seemed to be taking part in her meeting, and they paid no attention to her. She was considering the possibility that the invitation was a hoax and that was the end of it, when Trimble came up to her.

'You are to come with me,' he said shyly. He was a slightly older boy whom Millie did not know well, and she was surprised that he had been sent to fetch her. She followed him down the corridor, and unexpectedly into the prefects' room, where three older boys were sitting on chairs facing the door. They were ready for Millie, and Church, a senior prefect, stood up.

'Good afternoon, Millie. Welcome to our meeting.' They all watched her seriously, and she hoped that they had something more interesting to tell her, or perhaps they would show her a new invention, or maybe give her the key to a secret language.

'Please sit down at this desk.' he indicated a desk beside her, and she sat down facing the three senior boys. Trimble waited by the door, shifting uneasily, but there was no sign of the two boys who had sent the invitation. Church was the spokesman, and Barker and Hutchinson sat in heavy silence.

'We have formed a club, called the Supernaturalists Club,' Church said pompously, standing in front of the desk. 'We,' and he pointed to the other two boys, 'are the organizing committee.' Millie then noticed that the boys had round white badges pinned to their grey jackets, though she could not make out the words on them.

'We would like you to become a member.' He turned to a desk behind the chairs and picked up another badge. 'We confer this badge,' he began.

'The form,' Hutchinson interrupted in a whisper. 'The enrolment form.'

'Oh yes,' Church said quickly. 'We would like you to fill in a form first.' He picked up a sheet of paper from his desk and placed it in front of Millie. 'There are a few questions for you to answer.'

Millie looked blankly at the sheet of paper. 'I need a pencil,' she said, playing for time.

'Oh yes, a pencil,' Church said, flustered, and fumbled round his desk until he found one. He handed it to Millie and stood looking down while she still stared at the paper.

'I can't spell these words,' she said, pointing to the list of hand-written questions.

'Which ones?' Church said. 'You can do the first one, that's your name.'

Millie slowly and laboriously wrote 'm' 'i' 'l' 'l' 'i', and then she stopped. 'Do you want all my name?' she asked.

'Your full name,' Church said sternly, and Millie went on with 'c' 'e' 'n' 't' 'n' 'e' 'w' 'm' 'a' 'n'.

'That's enough, let's leave the form,' Hutchinson said impatiently. 'It's taking too long, we're going to be late.'

'You can complete the form later,' Church said, keeping up his pompous manner. 'I now confer this badge,' he went on, and looked round for the missing badge.

'It's on the desk,' Barker sneered. 'Get on with it.'

'Oh yes, here it is,' Church said, holding up the badge. 'With this badge I promote you to be a member of the Supernaturalists Club.' He carefully pinned the home-made badge to the front of Millie's dress, and she squinted down at it, wondering what powers it gave her.

'As a member of the Club,' Church said, standing back, 'you are entitled to meet supernatural beings. The sign for the Club is this.' He held up his hand with the palm facing Millie and lowered his middle finger. 'When you see someone make this sign, you know they are in communion with supernatural beings.'

'Communication,' Hutchinson muttered, but Church ignored the correction. Millie carefully copied his hand movements, and suddenly Barker and Hutchinson both stood up and made the sign, and Millie and the three boys silently faced each other, their hands held up stiffly in front of them. Millie peeped over her shoulder to see if Trimble was making the sign too, but he stood guarding the door and took no part in the ceremony.

'You are now initiated,' Church said, lowering his hand. Millie did not judge this to be the best time to ask what all the long words meant. She felt flattered, and she trusted that they would be explained to her later. She put her hand on her lap and waited.

Barker and Hutchinson both lowered their hands and looked at Church, and Church looked at Trimble. 'Trimble will now escort you to the Chief Wizard,' Church said to Millie, speaking over her head. 'That's all, you can go now.' His confidence had suddenly evaporated, and he was left with embarrassment. 'That's all,' he repeated, looking down at the floor.

Nobody moved, and Church became agitated. 'Get on with it Trimble, can't you?' He hopped from foot to foot and scowled at Trimble. 'Bloody buck up.'

Trimble came forward and Hutchinson said kindly to Millie, 'you may leave now,' and smiled and nodded.

'Is that all?' Millie said, dismayed. She had hoped they would explain a bit more before it was over.

'You are to meet the wizard,' Hutchinson said in a sickly sweet voice. Millie turned to Trimble for enlightenment, but he also looked embarrassed, and merely said gruffly, 'come on.' The three senior boys said nothing more, so Millie got up and followed Trimble out of the room.

In the corridor Trimble walked fast, not speaking to the few boys they passed, and Millie had to trot to keep up with him. He stopped abruptly at the entrance to the locker room and held out his arm.

'You must wait here,' he said to Millie. 'I have to check things first.' He went into the locker room, and Millie looked around for an ally, but there were none in sight.

'You can come in now,' he said, reappearing at her side. 'Come on.' He gently pulled at the sleeve of her dress and led her to the near corner of the locker room, out of sight of the doorway. The room was empty except for a strange sight in the corner. A boy stood with a large cardboard box on his head, with rough holes cut out for his eyes. The box was painted crudely in red and black stripes, and it wobbled unsteadily on his shoulders.

'Aaahhh,' a voice said from the box, sounding hollow and deep from the muffled interior. 'It is Millie Newman, is it not?' The box tilted so as to see her better, and then slowly nodded. 'So you have come to consult the Chief Wizard.' The voice spoke in grand sepulchral tones, and Millie could not recognize it, however hard she tried. The grey jacket and trousers underneath were anonymous, and all she could tell was that the boy was quite a lot bigger than she was.

'Do you believe in fairies?' the voice said menacingly.

'Yes,' Millie said, because this seemed to be expected of her.

'Good, very good,' the voice said slowly. 'I am glad to hear that.' The boy shifted his feet and clasped his hands in front of his chest. 'I am the Chief Wizard, and I am going to take you to meet the fairies.' There was a pause while there was some coughing and sniffing. 'The fairies have long wanted to meet a human, but it has to be a human who believes in them.' The box nodded very slowly. 'If you do not believe in them, they will disappear, and that would be very sad for them.' The boy rubbed his hands together. 'So you must believe in them very very hard. If you don't,' he paused and curled his hands in the shape of claws, shaking them at Millie. 'Grrrr. Poof. They might try to get their own back on you.'

'What could they do?' Millie asked nervously.

'They would creep in at night,' the voice said in a hollow whisper, 'and haunt you. Whoooo. Whoooo.' The voice ended with sinister owl-like cries.

'I believe in fairies,' Millie repeated meekly. In fact she had not made up her mind on the subject, but she was not happy with the turn of events and it seemed wiser to agree for the time being.

'Good. Let's go then.' The Wizard leapt into boy-like action, and the box shook so much that it was in danger of falling off. 'Trimble, lead the way.'

Millie was relieved that Trimble was to stay with them. He had become a pillar of normality compared to the strange behaviour she was meeting that afternoon, and she found his presence reassuring. She kept close to him as he went to the doorway.

'Wait,' he said, as he looked up and down the corridor, and then he waved them on. He and Millie started walking rapidly towards the gym, but they were stopped by muffled groans from the Wizard behind them.

'Not so fast you idiot. I can't keep up at that pace,' the voice complained and they waited while the Wizard shuffled forward to catch up with them, the box tilting to peer down at the floor, until the Wizard put his hand on Trimble's shoulder.

'You guide until we get outside,' the voice said, and Millie turned to take a closer look at him, as she nearly, but not quite, recognized him. The Wizard put his other hand on Millie's shoulder.

'We three will keep together,' the voice said in careful lugubrious tones. 'We go to meet the fairies.' They went forward in a close band, the boy with the box supported in the middle, until they reached the gym entrance, where they carefully negotiated the step outside to the wide back yard where the cars coming in from the drive could make a sweeping turn and depart. There were rarely visitors on a Wednesday afternoon, so Millie was not surprised to find the yard deserted now. But she did expect to meet a member of staff sooner or later, and as the tight little group moved forward she wondered what would happen when they confronted an adult. The Wizard would surely be exposed, and he would have difficulty explaining himself away. But coincidence was on the side of the fairies, and they crossed the yard and reached the bend of the drive without meeting anyone, either boy or adult. Turning the bend, they finally met Wilcox, who was clearly expecting them.

'About time too,' he said with relief. 'I was getting worried that something had gone wrong.' He turned politely to Millie. 'I am so glad that you can be with us. It gives great pleasure to the Wizard and me to introduce you to the fairies.' He stepped across the border of grass at the edge of the drive and opened the small wicket-gate in the fence round the top of the old orchard. 'They will be waiting for us. Thank you Trimble, that will be all.'

'Oh, can't Trimble come with us?' Millie burst out in alarm.

Wilcox shook his head. 'We're going to show you round, me and the Wizard. There wouldn't be room for Trimble as well. Anyway,' he added, 'the fairies don't like too many people at once.'

'Oh, please let Trimble come too,' Millie said urgently, but Trimble was already disappearing round the bend of the drive, running hard without looking back.

'He's gone now,' Wilcox stated. 'We go this way.' He stepped into the long grass of the orchard, and Millie, free of the Wizard's hand from her shoulder, nervously followed him, leaving the

Wizard teetering on the edge of the grass.

'Give us a hand, Wilcox,' the booming voice said, and the box rocked backwards and forwards.

Wilcox laughed. 'You're all right. Just walk straight ahead, there're no steps here.' The Wizard stumbled uncertainly in the grass, while Wilcox and Millie watched from the orchard. She was unsure who she could turn to for support now that the fleeting Trimble had gone, and perhaps there was no one she could rely on today. Sometimes one seemed to want to help her, and sometimes another, but in the end they all appeared changeable and unsafe. At the moment, though, it was the Wizard who looked the least threatening, and she turned to him.

'Here's the gate, this way,' she said gently, and she took his hand. The boy jumped, and the box swivelled to see who was leading him, but he kept hold of Millie while they made their way through the clumps of grass and caught up with Wilcox. They were now on a rough track which led through the top of the orchard to the most decrepit of the wooden sheds, which Millie knew was little used and near collapsing, with the weathered black wall-boards slipping and weeds pushing up between the gaps. The party of three followed the track in single file, with Wilcox leading, Millie close behind and the Wizard keeping an eye on their backs and confidently going where they went.

'One Two Three Approach Goblin,' Wilcox shouted loudly. 'That's the password,' he explained to Millie over his shoulder. 'They have to be ready for us, otherwise they might not come out and then we wouldn't see them.'

Millie was suddenly puzzled. 'But do fairies come out in the daytime?'

'Fairies are always out, aren't they, Mr. Chief Wizard,' he called to the back of the file.

'What did you say?' the Wizard replied, concentrating on the pathway.

'It's because the daylight is so bright,' Wilcox said to Millie, 'that we usually don't see the fairies. But they are there all the time. You can see them better in a dark place.'

This was a reasonable explanation to Millie and accounted for their approach to the ill-lit shed. She veered slightly towards a belief in fairies, though she still held a large reserve of doubt on the subject.

'One Two Three Approach Goblin,' Wilcox repeated, but more quietly this time. They were near the back of the shed, and they slowly picked their way through the nettles and brambles to reach the door at the front. They all three stopped at the entrance and peered expectantly into the dim interior. The door appeared to be stuck half open, and Millie could just make out the broken and dusty shelves, cluttered with discarded sacks and boxes. There was complete silence from inside the shed.

'I expect they want to see you better,' Wilcox whispered to Millie, as he stood close beside her. 'You go in a little way.' Millie tentatively pushed at the door, but it remained stuck. 'Go on, push a bit harder,' Wilcox urged, and Millie boldly stepped in and heaved her shoulder at the front edge of the door.

'Ow,' Millie shrieked, as something wet and cold hit the back of her neck and ran down inside her dress. She hunched her shoulders and put her hands over her face.

Wilcox was by her side at once. 'Dear me, dear me, what can it be.' He patted her back and took hold of her hand. 'There must be one of the naughty fairies around. I'll cast a spell to keep them away.' He faced the gloomy interior and intoned. 'Bad fairy, bad fairy, go away, go away. Never come back to this place today.' He patted her hand. 'There now, you're safe. You can go in now.'

'I don't want to,' Millie said in a small voice.

'You can't stop now,' Wilcox said indignantly. 'Having got this far, you might as well meet the good fairies, at least.' He gave her a little push in the back. 'Go on, they're expecting you.'

Millie edged round the door, and Wilcox, standing in the narrow entrance, blocked out almost all the light. She could hardly see any coherent object, and she put out her hands to feel the way, taking small shuffling steps into the dimness. She thought she heard a twitter, and then a squeak, coming from the dark corner behind the door, and she groped round in the cramped space.

108

'Did you see one?' Wilcox whispered, leaning in from the doorway.

'No,' Millie muttered. 'Where?' Immediately a dark feathery object brushed across her face and whisked away. 'Ow, ow,' she called out again, and she made a vain attempt to catch it.

'Was that one?' Wilcox said eagerly.

'I don't know,' she said miserably. 'It could have been a bat.' She wished to avoid bats, because she knew they got caught in girls' long hair, though it was unlikely they would lodge in her pigtails. She put a protective arm over her head, to be on the safe side, and swept the space in front of her with her other arm. Twitterings and squeaks started again from the corner, clearer this time, and she could just make out the feathery object jumping up and down below the roof.

'There you are, I'm sure that's one,' Wilcox said. Millie stood still and watched the object carefully. Her eyes were becoming used to the dim light, and the object flapped and jerked irregularly, looking to her more like a glove or torn handkerchief, without the substance of a body.

'Where's its head?' she said doubtfully, and the object wriggled ecstatically while the squeaks and twitters increased and multiplied, making an angry noise.

'Not all fairies have bodies like us,' Wilcox said. 'Some of them are merely spirits.'

'That's not what it says in my book,' Millie said firmly.

Wilcox laughed nervously. 'You can't always believe books. There are lots of different kinds of fairies, and this one is a Pixilated Elf, they're very rare.'

'I've never heard of that,' she said dismissively, watching the object closely because she thought she could see a string stretched above it. Suddenly another object brushed across the back of her head. This one was hard and cold and wet, and reminded her of the squashed frog.

'Aoowww,' she shrieked loudly, and immediately there was complete silence from the shed. Not a squeak or rustle came from the corner, and the black object flopped down onto a dusty shelf.

109

'Oh dear,' Wilcox said. 'You've frightened them away.' They both stood and listened. 'Yes, they've gone now. Never mind,' he said cheerfully. 'I'm sure you've done them no harm. They'll probably be back tomorrow.' He backed out of the shed. 'They were only little ones anyway. Let's leave this place now.' He leant forward and took hold of Millie's elbow. 'Come with me, I'll show you some bigger ones, you'll really like them.'

But Millie's curiosity had made her bolder, and she wanted time to inspect the phenomena and get to the bottom of the truth about fairies. She took a step further into the shed and kicked at a dirty sack.

'Don't do that,' Wilcox said agitatedly, and he grabbed harder at her arm and pulled her back. 'You mustn't do that, you might kill a fairy that's asleep in there.'

'Fairies don't sleep in sacks,' Millie said, but she was not able to pursue the argument because Wilcox clasped his arms tightly round her, lifted her off the ground and staggered backwards with her into the broad daylight. He dumped her down in front of the Wizard, who was busy adjusting his box on his shoulders.

'How did it go?' the Wizard said, sounding worried.

'I think we'd better move on,' Wilcox replied, and he sighed heavily. 'It's hard work, hunting for fairies. It's all right for you,' he added, laughing at the Wizard.

'Wad'you mean,' the Wizard replied indignantly, clasping his wobbling box, and he danced over to Wilcox. 'I'll put a spell on you,' he said in as low a voice as he could manage.

'Don't lose your head,' Wilcox said, and laughed at his own joke.

Millie lost interest in the boys when they started making their silly jokes, and she looked more closely at the unfamiliar section of the school grounds. It was certainly well hidden, behind the other sheds and protected by clumps of uncut brambles, and she was surprised she had not ventured here before. It seemed to be an area known to the boys, and it was true that there were not many places which remained hidden from the staff, so this would make it an attraction for them. Now that they were outside the shed, she was glad to be in the fresh air, and already she had no desire to return to the stuffy, mysterious dangers inside the shed, fairies or no fairies. She looked with distaste at the rotting corner boards, and then she thought she saw them move, bulging out and in again, with whispers coming from inside.

'That's nothing,' Wilcox shouted in a strange manner, seeing Millie staring at the shed. 'The shed is very old, it moves easily.' He was shouting much louder than was necessary for the short distance between him and Millie. 'We will be going now,' he went on, shouting each word clearly. 'Come on Wizard, come on Millie, we will climb through the fence.' He waved his hand to them in silence, seeming confused as to who he was talking to, and the Wizard swung his box backwards and forwards, trying to find out what was going on.

'This way, advance!' Wilcox finally yelled, and he ran to the broken-down fence between the orchard and the larger wooden sheds. The Wizard shuffled after him and Millie walked behind, catching up with the two boys as they waited at the fence.

'You must keep moving,' Wilcox said, his responsibilities making him irritable. 'The fairies only came here for you.' He spoke severely to Millie, and she became confused as to who was supposed to be doing whom a favour, she or the fairies, and it added to the strangeness of the afternoon.

They climbed easily through the broken gap in the fence, which brought them immediately to the smaller and more remote of the wooden sheds, kept in use and better repaired. There was even glass in the two small windows, high up in the side wall, and these were now propped open. The Wizard stopped by the side of the shed, bowed to Millie as low as he could without losing his box, and then held out his arm towards the shed.

'Silence. The Chief Wizard speaks,' Wilcox quickly said, standing behind Millie.

'Quite so,' the Wizard said importantly. 'Allow me to introduce you to the senior fairies of the district. We have reached their summer residence.' He waved his arm at the shed.

111

'We will announce our presence and wait for the sign that they wish to receive us.'

Millie looked round the corner at the door in the front of the shed, and found it shut. She had occasionally visited the shed, when it was always filled with musty vegetables, stored in sacks and boxes and hanging in bunches from the roof. It was well aired and cool, and she was surprised that fairies should choose a place that was neither cosy nor undisturbed.

'You must wait for the sign,' Wilcox said. 'You can't go in yet.'

'Don't they get frightened by the gardeners?' Millie asked.

'Oh bloody hell,' Wilcox said, exasperated by yet another question, and the Wizard actually giggled. 'I have no doubt that the fairies,' Wilcox sighed, 'send out spies to see who's coming.'

'Then they know we are here,' Millie said reasonably. They all three stood silently outside the shed, but no sign was given to indicate the presence of the fairies.

'You call them up,' Wilcox said enthusiastically to Millie. 'You call out that you want to see them.'

'Shall I say the password?' Millie asked.

'Say something nice,' the Wizard said, 'what you think they'd like to hear.'

Millie thought for a moment. 'Hello,' she said, not very loudly, but there was still no reply.

'Try again,' Wilcox said.

'Hello,' Millie repeated, louder. 'Hello, hello.' They waited in silence.

Suddenly there was a dreadful scream, and a round black hairy object popped out from the bottom of the shed wall and rattled backwards and forwards. Millie jumped back in alarm, tripped over Wilcox's feet and was prevented from falling by Wilcox clasping her in his arms. The Wizard also seemed surprised and backed away from the shed, and the three of them stared at the wall as the screams continued from inside the shed. Millie just had time to notice that the agitated hairy object was on the end of a stick, coming out through a hole in the wall, when there were many more bangs, groans and screams from the shed, and a host of objects, white, long, feathery, round, red, large and small, came rattling out on sticks through the open windows and flapped and banged and twisted.

'Are these fairies?' Millie asked, wriggling away from Wilcox to move further back.

'Yes, yes,' Wilcox replied, 'they're the bigger ones.'

'They didn't like what you said,' the Wizard called out to Millie over the din.

'I only said Hello,' Millie replied indignantly, and this brought screams from the shed so unearthly that Millie was quite frightened. Could this sound be made by boys? Or by fairies? If she could find out who was at the end of the sticks, then the mystery would be settled once and for all. The windows were not so very high, and she started jumping up and down to see inside.

'Careful,' Wilcox said.

'I want to see the fairies,' Millie explained, expecting to be fobbed off with another excuse for their invisibility. But to her surprise Wilcox at once put his arms round her stomach and gently lifted her up until her head was almost level with the windows. They stood out of range of the shaking objects, and Millie looked past them, through the dusty glass to the dark interior. She could see the sticks going in, catching the light as they shook, and then, abruptly, nothing, only blackness. She put her hand on Wilcox's shoulder and tried to lever herself higher, and Wilcox staggered backwards.

'I can't hold you if you do that,' he said, puffing with discomfort.

'I can't see,' Millie said, with a mixture of alarm and dissatisfaction. 'I can only see black.'

'Have one more look,' he said, and eased forwards again. She stared in bewilderment at the rattling objects, the cobwebby windows, the shaking sticks, and then the blackness. Nothing was settled, she thought gloomily, as she listened to screams more hideous than she had ever heard before.

'Put me down,' she said resignedly.

'That was one of the best displays I've seen,' Wilcox said, as he slid her down to the ground. 'They must really like you, to come out in force like that.' Millie looked doubtfully at the shed, where the rattles and screams continued unabated. 'They don't do that for just anyone,' Wilcox went on. 'Well done, Millie.' He slapped her heartily on the back, and if she had not been so overwhelmed by the dilemma presented to her by the conflicting evidence, proving either the existence of fairies or the trickery of boys, then she would have been considerably prouder of so much commotion entirely on her account.

'They are getting tired,' Wilcox said, though the continuing noise did not bear him out. The Wizard had already walked round to the path in front of the shed, and he was nervously waiting by the shed door.

'Come on,' he called out, and then he shot back and bumped in-to Wilcox. 'Quick,' he said, with breathless urgency. 'You go on. I'll wait here behind the shed.'

Wilcox immediately took command again. 'That will be enough for today.' He put his arm round Millie's shoulders and walked her firmly and speedily to the path leading to the other garden sheds. 'We will leave them to have a rest now.'

'Where's the Wizard?' Millie looked back and saw the apparently innocuous wooden shed, standing still and now silent by the orchard fence, with no one in sight. But she would not trust dark and dusty interiors again, with their capacity to burst into fearful mysteries.

'He's doing something,' Wilcox said vaguely, and he pointed to the badge on the front of Millie's dress. 'It was your badge that did it. They knew you were a member of the Club.' They both looked down at the badge as they walked along, and they were thus surprised by finding Taverner on the path in front of them.

'Hey, hey,' Taverner said, and then roared with laughter. 'So you've found your sweetheart, have you.' Millie looked up crossly, not being in the mood for jokes on that troublesome afternoon, and Wilcox tightened his grip round her shoulders, willing her to silence.

'We were going for a peaceful walk, thank you, Taverner,' Wilcox said firmly and grandly, in a manner suitable for conversing with under-gardeners. 'Millie had some questions which I was helping her with.' But this explanation did not quieten Taverner at all. On the contrary, he held his sides and half collapsed with laughter, rocking across the path and preventing Wilcox from pushing past.

'Oh, oh, some questions, oh, oh,' Taverner gasped. 'Tell that to the marines.' He suddenly lurched forwards and tweaked Wilcox's ear. 'Tut, tut, was it questions about the birds and the bees?'

'Oh, stuff it, Taverner.' Even Wilcox was now cross, and he tried to sidle past, pulling Millie with him. But Taverner was still filled with his delight and he would not let them go.

'I won't tell, my boy.' He rocked from side to side in front of them. 'You can trust me, my sweethearts, I can keep a secret.'

'For Christ's sake shut up'. Wilcox let go of Millie and took a swipe at Taverner with his arm, which missed by a long way.

'Now, now, don't lose your temper,' Taverner said, stepping back and grinning all the more.

Wilcox stood still and scowled. 'Don't be so silly, Taverner,' he said in precise tones, regaining his composure, and he beckoned to Millie. 'Let us leave this foul-minded creature.' Taverner stood by the side of the path and roared with laughter, and Wilcox passed in front of him with as much dignity as he could muster. 'I hope you choke in the stink of your own putrefaction,' he added as a parting shot.

Taverner giggled and jerked his thumb at Wilcox. 'You've picked a brainy one there,' he said to Millie, as she stood waiting nervously for the menfolk to settle their altercation. She stepped cautiously past Taverner and then ran to catch up with Wilcox as he strode on haughtily.

'Ta ta,' he called out behind them. 'Sweet dreams.'

'Ignore him,' Wilcox muttered grimly to Millie at his side. But Millie was not sure which side she was on, and she turned round to look again at Taverner's reassuring smile. He grinned and shook his fist in a sturdy gesture, and she gave a small wave in return.

'He's got no right to speak like that,' Wilcox said crossly to Millie as they walked on. 'You shouldn't have anything to do with him. He causes a lot of trouble with his unpleasantnesses.'

'He's always been nice to me,' Millie said thoughtfully.

'The trouble with you,' Wilcox said firmly, 'is that you don't understand.'

The trouble with everyone, Millie thought wearily, as they crossed the drive towards the gym entrance, is that no one will explain anything. It would be a relief to have one puzzle settled that afternoon, and there was not much time left.

'Tell me,' she said urgently. 'Are fairies really real?'

Wilcox paused for a long time, looking down at the gravel as they walked across the yard. Millie could hear the high chatter of the boys as they gathered in the corridor ahead of them, waiting for the supper bell. A few were following them across the yard, and Wilcox would soon be one of the mob. He took a deep breath and looked at Millie. 'What do you think?' he said with half a knowing smile.

Millie looked him in the eye with a stern challenge. 'Tell me,' she said crossly. He blinked miserably, troubled by his conflicting loyalties.

'You'll have to find out for yourself,' he said grimly, and then, as two small boys ran past them and nipped in through the gym entrance, he added, 'you did see them, after all, didn't you?' Millie shook her head in despair, and he said quickly, 'I mean, you have the evidence, you must decide for yourself.'

'That's what I mean,' she said pleadingly. 'Are they real?' They stepped in through the entrance and were confronted by the noisy corridor filled with groups of boys moving towards the dining room end. Wilcox suddenly bent down to Millie.

'Don't trust boys,' he whispered hotly in her ear. 'They're up to no good.'

'What?' Millie said, startled. But Wilcox had become a prefect again, smiling and distant. He waved his hand towards the door of the prefects' room. 'Do you want to say goodbye to the organizing committee?'

'Oh no,' Millie said, horrified. She had had enough of boys for that day. 'There'll be a row already because I've missed my tea.'

'Very well then.' Wilcox stopped at the door. 'Thank you for your attendance.' He stood awkwardly to one side while boys jostled past, and Millie was pushed first on one side then on the other by the eager stream of boys. He gave a polite dismissive wave of his hand, and Millie concentrated on fighting her lone way through the grey-clad mass of hungry, vociferous, self-absorbed, impatient schoolboys.

9

The time for action had now come, of this Millie was certain, as she reflected in her room in the evening. She lay in bed and looked at the more complex words which replaced the letters pinned round the wall. The struggle with 'know' and 'bough' and 'climb' would not be in vain. All her skills would be called into use, even knot-tying for lassoes. The episode with the fairies had stirred in her a challenge, and she would triumph over the whole world, over boys, adults, masters, staff, Taverner, Miss Ellen, Miss West, the English master, visiting parents, new boys, Alan and Alan's baby sister. She would need weapons and allies and, above all, planning, but with her accumulated wisdom derived from her observations and hard work, she should be able to achieve all her requirements. She would make a start next day, and she felt a frisson of exhilaration at her decision.

She lost no time in the morning, and before lessons started she sought out her father in his study and obtained his permission to have one boy to tea on Sunday, and furthermore she got him to write Fezel's name clearly on a piece of paper, and then, leaning heavily over the end of the large desk, she wrote below the name, 'please come to tea on Sunday', all the words neat and correct.

'Hurry along,' her father said. 'Classes will be starting.' She took her piece of paper and walked cautiously up the corridor, watching the boys file into their classrooms. She found the room with the junior boys, already at their desks and alarmingly noisy without a master present, and she was hesitating at the entrance when the English master came up behind her.

'Want to join us, Millie?' he said jokingly.

She held up her paper. 'Could you give this to Fezel,' she said authoritatively.

He took the paper and read it slowly. 'It doesn't say who it is from,' he said, still looking at the paper.

'You can tell him it's from me, can't you?' she said plaintively. He ignored her reply and strode into the classroom, and immediately Millie heard the concerted scrape of chairs as the boys stood up, and the chant of 'Morning Sir' in unison from the boys. She could only see the front two rows of boys and the master's desk from her position at the door. The English master stood by his desk, his chin up, looking down at his class. 'Good morning boys. Sit down. Except you, Fezel. You come up here.' Fezel appeared in the centre gangway, and a murmur arose from the class. The English master banged his hand on his desk. 'That's enough. Quiet everybody.' He looked at Fezel standing in front of him and handed him the paper without saying a word. 'Go and sit down,' he shouted, his only method of speech when in front of the class. 'Now we can get on with some work. Wellington, close the door.'

Millie moved away quickly and trotted towards the green baize door and her own lessons. She was confident that Fezel would accept the invitation, as she knew that the boys prized such a treat, and she particularly wanted him because he was more likely to tell the truth. His bursts of grand manner had made him slightly unpopular among the boys, and there was a greater chance that he would tell on the others, when Millie so required it.

Indeed, when Sunday came, Fezel turned up punctually in the afternoon in Millie's room. He had sent no word, but everyone had assumed that he would be there. Miss Case had laid out tea for two on the table, and Miss Ellen had decided that with such diminished numbers, she did not need to stay in the room. However, she was present for Fezel's arrival, and she warned them that she would pop in from time to time from her near-by watch-out in the sewing room.

Once alone, Millie and Fezel were pleasantly subdued, having no need to defend or compete. They started by inspecting the food on the table, and Millie, wishing to keep Fezel in a good

119

mood, was inspired to become a hostess.

'Please try one of these,' she said sweetly, grasping a plate of buns and carefully lifting it up towards him. 'I know they are delicious.'

'Have you had them before?' Fezel said as he took one. She carefully put the plate down. 'Only on Sundays,' she said, taking one herself.

'Sunday is a very special day,' Fezel said thoughtfully. 'You have different food, we do different things.' He looked sadly at the bun. 'In my country we have good food all the time, not just on one day.'

Millie looked round at the paste sandwiches and the two bowls of prunes and custard. It was certainly not a birthday tea. 'What is supper like in the dining room?' she asked.

'All right, I suppose,' he said without interest. 'The worst things about Sunday,' he said more emphatically, 'is Assembly. It's terrible,' he groaned and screwed up his face. 'It's absolutely terrible. They shouldn't be allowed to say such things. In my country they would be shot for saying such things.'

Such words of dissidence were music in Millie's ears, and she egged him on by pushing a slice of plum-cake towards him. 'Is it very bad? What do they say?'

'It's Merryman who takes Assembly. He's terrible. He mumbles half the time, and he goes on and on, and he's so absolutely boring. And you have to sit absolutely still, if you move an inch he'll start on his "attention is the schoolboy's first rule" lecture.'

'What else does he say?'

'Lies, lies, it's all lies. He says things like "pleasure-seeking leads to vanity and emptiness," and "a Christian gives thanks and does not grumble," Well, you've only got to look at old Merryman to see that it's not true.' Millie listened enraptured. 'Then he says things like "wars are due to men's wickedness." Well, I know that that's nonsense, because you've got to fight for your beliefs, haven't you? Then do you know what he said last Sunday?' Millie shook her head. 'He said that children suffer the

120

sins of their parents.' Fezel glowered furiously. 'The bloody fool. He doesn't know what he's talking about.' Millie started to snigger, but then stifled the urge when she saw Fezel's awesome glint of rage. 'He's a bloody idiot. He should be strung up, or, or . . .' Fezel was overcome by his frustrations.

'We could invent a torture,' Millie said enthusiastically, thinking of her adventure book, and then she remembered a history story. 'He could be hung drawn and quartered.'

Fezel smiled. 'They don't do that now.' Millie's excesses had calmed him. 'All the same, there should be some way of shutting him up. He shuffles around, with a silly smile, and he's really really old.' Fezel looked seriously at Millie. 'It would even be better if your father took Assembly.'

'Do you think so?' Millie said, surprised. If her father was an improvement, then the tedium of Merryman's lectures must be extreme.

'Your father's quite nice to the boys, he doesn't give beatings or shout, and he's good at cricket, and he doesn't go on about Christianity.' This gave Millie a new slant on her father, and she remained thoughtful.

'Your father doesn't lie either,' Fezel added.

'How do you know?' Millie said, surprised at this compliment.

'That's what all the boys say, he's never let anyone down.' Fexel smiled. 'He's never been caught out in a lie, anyway, and that's what counts.' He laughed, his cheerful spirits returned.

Millie smiled too, as she was enjoying this new view of her father.

'Do you understand jometry?' she asked.

'It's all right. Not bad,' Fezel said. 'I tell you what's really good.'

'What's that?' Millie prompted.

'Art,' Fezel said. Millie was most surprised, as Art had not come within her list of subjects. She knew that every afternoon the end classroom became a messy room, with paints and paste and water and paper, but she had never seen any use for the end products, and they did not feature in her Plan. Now she reconsidered Art, and it gave her an idea.

'Did you see a boy making a sort of helmet, like a box with holes in and paint all over it?' Millie asked hopefully.

'No,' Fezel said. 'No one's done anything like that.'

'Are you sure?' Millie said, disappointed.

'Nobody's made anything for going on the head,' he repeated. 'But I've moulded a horse, out of paper mashay, it's really good, it's rearing up and I've painted it black and white, and I'll take it home in the holidays and show it to my father.'

Millie had now come round, obliquely, to her main subject. 'Could you mould a fairy?' she asked quietly.

'I wouldn't want to,' Fezel said simply.

She tried again, from a different angle. 'Did you know the boys had sent me an invitation, and they took me to a club and a wizard and all that?'

'Oh that,' Fezel said disparagingly, and he threw back his head and folded his arms. 'That was the business set up by Brown May.'

'Brown Ma?' Millie said. 'He wasn't there.'

'He started it, though,' Fezel said. 'With Masseau. They were furious, you see, because you'd put them on a list for tea and then you'd chosen someone else.'

'But I'd never invited Brown Ma,' Millie said indignantly.

'No, but you'd invited Brown Mi, and that's the same thing.'

'But I explained that I wasn't allowed to have them all, I was only allowed three.'

'Well, you didn't choose them, did you?' Fezel said smugly. 'You see,' he went on, and then paused, 'how can I explain it to you?' He put his elbows on the table and rested his chin on his fists. 'It is something special to be asked to tea, everyone wants to be asked, and then when you didn't choose them, they were very cross, and then they said they would invite you to something else in return. You see? That's what it was.'

Millie waited for more, and then she said, 'but what did they invite me to?'

'Oh, I don't know about that,' he said dismissively. 'It was

122

something outside, wasn't it? You went, you should know.'

'But I want to know who did it all, who fixed it, who, who did it?' she persisted.

'I don't know exactly,' Fezel explained. 'I know Brown Ma and Masseau thought it up, and then Brown Ma went to the prefects, and then they arranged it all. I didn't have anything to do with it,' he added.

Millie looked across the tea table at Fezel, his head resting on his hand, and she knew that he had done his best. 'What will happen to you,' she said, suddenly worried, 'now that you have been to tea two times?'

'They'll rag me a bit, I expect,' he said casually.

'Won't you mind?' She was impressed with his loyalty.

'It won't last for long,' he said. 'They forget pretty quickly. Anyway.' He stopped and leant across the table. 'Can you keep a secret?'

'Yes. Of course,' she whispered eagerly.

'You know I am a Prince.' He spoke very seriously.

'Yes,' Millie said.

'A Crown Prince.' He spoke slowly.

'Yes,' Millie said again.

'There are some boys here,' he lowered his voice, 'who want to depose me.'

Millie was very impressed, although she did not know what it meant. 'What will they do?' she whispered.

'I'm sure it's been started,' he narrowed his eyes, 'by the Jews.'

'What's that?' Millie said sharply. She did not want to deal with another mystery.

'Some of the boys are Jews. You knew that, didn't you?' He was becoming aggressive.

'Yes, yes,' she said, to quieten him down.

'I came across a plot.' He waved his hand. 'It's too complicated to explain it to you. But my father will send guards if it goes any further.'

'Really?' Millie said, impressed again.

He nodded and stood up. 'You mustn't tell anybody about

123

this.' He stared severely at her.

'Of course not,' Millie said, filled with admiration.

'It might have international percussions.' He still fixed her with his eye.

Millie breathed deeply, controlling her nervous excitement. 'Can I help?' She saw herself carrying messages at night and handing them to dark figures. 'Will the guards wear uniforms?' They would no doubt be stationed about the grounds, or in corners of the school building, and they would take tea in the pantry.

'It's not like that,' Fezel said, not unkindly. 'You'll understand when you are bigger.' He smiled thoughtfully. 'Perhaps you can visit my country one day.'

Millie sighed. It was all too far away for her, and there were enough events within the grounds in need of explanation. Could they be linked? She frowned anxiously. 'Are there spies from your country in the school?'

Fezel shook his head. 'No, no, it doesn't work like that. It's really too complicated to explain.' He leant his hands on the table and looked down seriously at Millie, and she thought he looked more like a prince than ever. 'In my country there is a whole department for security, they look like ordinary men, but underneath they are very very clever. And they can shoot, too,' he added gravely.

Millie was not so happy with his country after all, and its glamour was decreasing as its threat increased. She concentrated on more immediate problems. 'Let's practice making lassoes again,' she said brightly, and wriggled out of her chair.

Fezel put his hands in his pockets. 'There's not enough room in here, you can't swing it properly.'

'You can show me knots,' she said happily. 'You know some knots, don't you?' She fetched her newly collected pieces of string and held them out to him.

'What's this?' he said, holding up a cord with a heavy lead ball at the end.

'The builders left it,' she said briefly. 'It's very strong.'

124

'I'll show you a slip-knot,' he said, gaining enthusiasm. 'Then I'll show you the knots we use for the horses.'

They each selected string and worked hard at making and re-making all the knots he knew. Miss Ellen, looking in for a moment, saw only quiet concentration and was fully content. Millie enjoyed the skill of manipulating string, and Fezel showed her a cat's-cradle. She found the different string patterns fascinating, and she wanted to continue for ever, but when the time came for Fezel to leave for prep hour, she did not detain him, because she now knew that his letter writing was of international importance.

After he had gone she slipped out quickly, leaving Miss Ellen uninterrupted in the sewing room, and she skipped down to the pantry. Sunday was an irregular day in the pantry, and she was not sure whom she would find there. To her pleasure, Hamble and Mrs. Hamble were sitting at the table quietly drinking tea, and they gave her a big welcome.

'Millie, my dear. You look prettier than ever.' Mrs. Hamble smiled warmly and lifted her hands in zealous admiration.

'It's my Missie Millie,' Hamble said, getting up. 'Why now, you can take a cup of tea with us.'

'It's quite a little time since we saw you last,' Mrs. Hamble said, smiling sweetly while she inspected Millie. 'I do believe you've grown a tiny bit.'

Millie edged round the table until she came to the chair next to Hamble, then she sat down and gave her sweetest smile across the table to Mrs. Hamble. 'I'm six now,' she said, giving the chatter that she knew would keep Mrs. Hamble happy. 'And this is my new summer dress, it's the first time I've worn it, and look, it's got a proper belt.' She pulled at the shiny white belt, but it was well below the level of the table, and Mrs. Hamble merely smiled and nodded.

'Now here's your cuppa,' Hamble said, leaning over Millie and placing a smart cup and saucer patterned with pink rosebuds in front of her. 'And why not, since it's such a special day, why not help yourself to sugar.' He placed a matching bowl, filled with lumps of sugar, next to the cup.

Millie grinned and twisted round to look up at him. 'Can I use the sugar tongs?'

'Why now.' Hamble clapped his hands. 'Quite right, that's a proper little lady.' He swung round and opened the cupboard behind him, and Mrs. Hamble laughed.

'You do have some funny little ways,' she said and shook her head. 'It must be living in a school that does it. Children need a home atmosphere.'

'Millie has all the boys for her playfellows, don't you, Missie Millie?' Hamble said, addressing his wife through Millie. He placed the sugar tongs with a flourish in the bowl, and patted Millie on the head. 'Away you go now, take as many as you want.'

'It's not rough boys that is best for little girls,' Mrs. Hamble said darkly.

'Come now,' Hamble said, returning to his chair. 'She has many privileges, and many friends. She doesn't do so badly.'

'She'll grow into a tomboy,' Mrs. Hamble said, 'and forget her manners.'

Millie ignored the conversation, and carefully manipulated the tongs, squeezing them round a lump of sugar.

'She may have high spirits, but she's got a warm heart,' Hamble said. 'That's my girl, Millie, you keep trying.'

Millie slowly lifted the sugar until it was above the tea cup, and then she released the tongs so that the sugar dropped into the tea with a large splash. The Hambles both laughed, and Mrs. Hamble said, 'never mind the marks,' referring to the drops of tea that had fallen on the tablecloth. Millie decided to repeat the performance, and she started again at the sugar bowl.

'My oh my,' Hamble said. 'You've got a sweet tooth today.' Millie concentrated on the tongs and added the second lump of sugar to her tea without mishap. She smiled proudly at Hamble as she put down the tongs.

'Now you give it a good stir with your spoon,' Hamble said.

126

'And you'll have a delicious cuppa tea.'

'Oh, no,' Millie said, dismayed. 'I don't want to stir it. I don't like it too sweet.'

They both laughed again, and Mrs. Hamble said, 'well I never,' and Hamble said, 'there's a girl who knows her own mind.' Millie cautiously took a sip of the tea, but abruptly replaced the cup on the saucer when she found it was still too hot to drink.

'Let it cool awhile,' Hamble said. 'A good cup is never spoiled by waiting.' Millie ignored this bewildering statement, as she judged it was a suitable moment to ask her question.

'What's a Jew?' she said, and immediately realized that she had stepped into forbidden territory. Both the Hambles stiffened and frowned uncomfortably. Mrs. Hamble stared at her tea cup, and Hamble spoke more sternly than usual to Millie.

'Who's been talking? Where did you hear this, then?'

Millie knew that she must tread carefully. 'I heard someone say that there was a Jew in the school.'

'Was it the boys who were saying this?' Hamble seemed unnecessarily cross.

'Yes,' Millie replied. 'It was the boys.'

'Who were they calling a Jew, do you know? Who were they talking about?' Hamble had become distressingly fierce, almost shouting, and Millie wished that she had not trusted her question to him. 'Come on now, come on, who's accused of being a Jew?'

'I don't know,' Millie wailed. 'I don't know. That's what I was asking you.'

'You're frightening her,' Mrs. Hamble snapped.

'Oh dear oh dear.' Hamble took a deep breath and let out the air with a hiss. 'I don't mean to upset you. But I have a bit of a temper, you see.' He shook his head self-importantly. 'We're only human, when all's said and done. I lived through the war, and fought, and suffered.'

'Steady, dear,' Mrs. Hamble warned.

Hamble turned on his wife. 'The things I saw on the battlefield, I tell you, I will never forget as long as I live.' He swung back to Millie. 'And the war was fought over the Jews. They held the power, they held the money, they've got a lot to answer for, even though they didn't start the shooting.'

'She's too young to understand that kind of talk,' Mrs. Hamble said scornfully.

'How do you tell a Jew?' Millie asked. She might as well pursue the subject, now that Hamble had controlled his temper.

'Aha,' Hamble said joyfully. 'Aha, aha. That's a very good question. Sometimes you can tell a Jew by his appearance, and sometimes you can't.'

'What does a Jew look like?' Millie continued.

'They've got black curly hair.' Hamble waved his hand in front of his face and laughed. 'And a big hooked nose.'

Millie looked at him thoughtfully. 'Fezel's got a big nose. And black hair.'

Hamble roared with laughter. 'Well, he's not a Jew, I can tell you.' He grinned gleefully. 'With Jews, you see, sometimes they look just like us and then you can't tell the difference.'

'So how do you tell a Jew?' Millie went on relentlessly.

'It's their religion,' Hamble said vaguely, and Mrs. Hamble nodded in agreement.

'They go to a different kind of church,' she explained, 'and they have different beliefs.'

Millie ignored this deviation and came to the point. 'So how can I tell who's a Jew in the school?'

The Hambles smiled at each other, and Millie had the familiar feeling of being excluded from a subject so vast and deep that she despaired of ever reaching the age when the full knowledge was hers and she could conquer the mysteries. She watched Hamble as he chose his words.

'It is difficult to tell,' he said slowly. 'Some of the boys are Jews, I have to admit, but you can really only tell by knowing who their parents are.'

'Can you tell?' Millie said, though she was tiring of the subject.

'I have some idea.' Hamble nodded thoughtfully. 'Some idea. I think I know pretty well which ones are the Jews. But,' he whispered portentously, leaning forward and pointing at Millie.

128

'I'm not telling you, in case you spread it around.'

This did not surprise Millie, but she had one more question. 'Why do the Jews not like Fezel?' she asked, and this produced an even more uncomfortable reaction than before. Both the Hambles shifted in their chairs, and Mrs. Hamble occupied herself with stacking the tea cups. Hamble drew in his breath with a hissing sound, and frowned at Millie.

'So where did you get that from? Has Prince Fezel been telling you stories?'

'Oh no.' Millie wished to keep Fezel as an ally, and she had promised him silence. 'I just wondered.' She decided some elaboration was needed. 'I heard the prefects talking about it, that's all.' She smiled sweetly to make the lie more acceptable, but Hamble's expression remained doubtful. 'They invited me to a treat,' she said cheerfully, to introduce a change of subject.

'Did they now.' Hamble smiled at last. 'And what kind of a treat was that?'

It was Millie's turn to become uncomfortable. The memories of the muffled voice in the box and the cold wet frog on her neck and the shrieking sticks and Taverner's smirks were all increasingly distasteful, and she resented the suspicion that she had been made a fool of. She gloomily watched her tea cup as it was removed by Mrs. Hamble, and she remained silent. Hamble laughed. 'It can't have been much of a treat, with you pulling a long face like that.' He watched her carefully. 'Tell me now, exactly what did the prefects say?'

'About the treat?' Millie said disingenuously.

'Ah no no. I'm asking what they said about Fezel.'

Millie casually shrugged her shoulders. 'Just that. They said the Jews didn't like him.' She also watched Hamble carefully for his reaction. 'They didn't say why,' she added.

Hamble shook his head gravely. 'This is a particularly serious matter, and above all coming from the prefects.'

'Boys will be boys,' Mrs. Hamble said, as she put the cups on the draining board.

Hamble turned in his chair to speak to her. 'We don't want

that kind of trouble in the school, and we must nip it in the bud. I shall have to consider reporting this.'

Millie felt a flutter of excitement at the thought that she might get the prefects into trouble, and she held her lips tight so that no squeak of joy could escape. Getting her own back on the prefects was an unexpected bonus, after she had received no help from any side on the long list of unexplained mysteries.

'You must do what you think best,' Mrs. Hamble said and looked up at the large wall-clock. 'Millie my dear, isn't it your bedtime?'

Hamble leapt up, clapped his hands and raced round the table. 'You'll be getting us into trouble, my Missie Millie. Quick, quick, look lively, up you go.' He spun round and darted to her side. 'Be a good girl,' he whispered, and patted her on the head.

Millie laughed happily and stood up. 'Thank you very much for the tea,' she said politely.

Hamble leant over and whispered again. 'Don't tell your Miss Ellen who it was that kept you late.'

Mrs. Hamble laughed. 'Don't put such ideas into her head.' She smiled at Millie. 'You're a truthful little girl, aren't you?'

'Oh yes,' Millie said with enthusiasm.

'I wouldn't suggest a real lie for Miss Ellen,' Hamble said, smiling, in his defence. 'Only a small white one.'

'What's a white lie?' Millie said in amazement, and sighed. All this time there was a hidden species of permissable lies, and she had never discovered them.

'You mustn't confuse her,' Mrs. Hamble said. 'A lie's a lie.'

'And we mustn't keep you any longer,' Hamble said, giving Millie another small pat on the head. 'Or we'll all be telling great big fibs instead of white lies.'

'Why's it white?' Millie said, though she hardly expected an answer.

'Now you've started something,' Mrs. Hamble sounded cross. 'Let her go up to bed.'

'Is it like a pretend one?' Millie said, still perplexed.

'Enough of all that.' Hamble suddenly knelt down beside

Millie and bowed his head. 'Jump up on my back. I'll give you a piggy-back up the stairs.' Millie paused, looking at the unfamiliar black-coated back in front of her. 'Hurry up,' he said, waving his arm backwards. 'Come on, jump up.'

Millie put her arms round his neck, and immediately he grasped her legs and rose up. Millie felt a splendid exhilaration at her great height, and she grinned down at Mrs. Hamble. 'Good night, Mrs. Hamble, good night,' she called out, and she clung with her fists under Hamble's chin as they jogged away.

10

A boxing match had been arranged for the Saturday of Half Term. Merryman had organized it all, as he considered it would provide a good rallying point for the boys who remained at the school. Many of the boys had gone home for the weekend, and others were out for the day with visiting relatives, and there was an air of lassitude throughout the building and the grounds. To counteract the danger of turpitude, Merryman had gathered a group from those boys who remained and persuaded them to take part in the boxing display, and furthermore he had gone round and whipped up an audience of sorts. The boys were none too keen on boxing, as they preferred their more vigorous and unsupervised fist fights in the locker room. For Merryman, boxing was the supreme sport, incorporating fitness, mental alertness, companionship, skilled defence and controlled aggression, and he regretted its decline in the school.

The gym had been provided with four metal-bound holes in the floor into which posts could be inserted to support a rope, thus forming a boxing ring at one end of the gym. Miss West had helped Merryman put out a few rows of chairs for the oddly-assorted audience, and she was trying to calm the remonstrating group of boys who were waiting against the wall. Merryman had ordered them to strip to the waist, and they stood in their games' shorts and plimsolls and complained of the cold. He had also paired them for the fights, but they maintained that they were unevenly matched and they could sort themselves out better. Miss West quietened them, re-paired them and told them to put on their games' shirts until it was their turn. She then waited while Merryman brought the boxing gloves, as only he was allowed to perform the ritual of pulling the heavy brown gloves

132

over the boys' hands and carefully tightening the laces. After the first two were ready gloved, the others had to wait, because there were not enough gloves except for those fighting, and furthermore with the different sized boys the gloves did not always give a good fit, though this was not a great disadvantage as the boys' proficiency at boxing was minimal.

Millie had been brought to watch the boxing match by her mother, and they sat in the middle of the front row. A few parents came in, wishing to support a school function, and her mother kept turning round to greet them and to say a few words to those sitting behind her. Millie looked round at everybody. She was surprised to see Mr. Green and Alan sitting in the back row. It was unusual for an employee to attend a school display, and she had never seen Alan in the school building before. Merryman had obviously been very active in drawing in his meagre audience. She saw the English master with some other members of staff, and she saw Matron at the end of the front row with Cook, to her astonishment. The two portly women seemed to be enjoying themselves more than anybody, as they smiled and nodded and muttered to each other. Fezel was sitting in the audience. He had refused to box, and there were other boys who had been rejected on grounds of poor sight, weak limbs or a lack of seriousness.

Merrymen stooped uncomfortably under the rope and stood up in the ring to face the audience. He was wearing an open-necked shirt and shorts, because not only was he the Ring Manager but he was also the Referee. Millie stared in wonderment at his lumpy knees, normally hidden by long trousers. Did he have other parts which were unexpectedly lumpy? She looked across at the waiting boys with their slender legs and their smooth skin, and she decided that she much preferred them. Merryman was going bald, too, and this was yet more distasteful.

Merryman smiled at the audience, clearly pleased with himself and announced the first contestants, reading from a list which he had taken from his pocket. He was immediately corrected by a chorus of waiting boys, and he stared at them in confusion until he understood what was going on. Then he called out the two correct names to the audience, as if there had never been a mistake, and two shivering boys bent under the rope and stood meekly before him. Merryman dropped the list which fluttered to the ground in front of Millie, bent his knees and flexed his elbows.

'Shake hands,' he hissed at the boys. 'And then go to your corners.' The boys clumsily touched with their gloves, jerked them up and down, and then shuffled backwards to opposite sides of the ring. Merryman drew out of his pocket a heavy stop-watch on a cord which he hung round his neck, and then he pulled out a whistle with a ribbon which he attached to his shirt button. The boys waited with their ungainly gloves hanging by their sides while Merryman started the stop-watch and blew the whistle. At once it was Merryman who pounced from foot to foot, held out his arms to balance himself and peered forward with lowered head.

'Come on,' he called out. 'Put up your guard. Start punching.' The boys crept forward, raised their gloves to their faces and eyed each other warily. 'Punch, punch,' he hissed at them, and they started wildly flinging out their arms. 'That's better, go on,' he urged, and he ran round to the other side. He had his back to Millie, and she could hear his heavy breathing, only a short distance in front of her, as he jogged from side to side. 'Aim your punches, don't waste them, go on, try harder, harder, that's better, your guard now, don't forget your guard.' He was panting out instructions to them all the time between his puffs of breath. Millie idly watched the flop of his buttocks as he jumped up and down.

Suddenly one of the boys cried out, staggered backwards for a few steps and clumsily held his glove to his nose. The other boy stood still, his gloves motionless at his sides, and Merryman ran round them again. 'Keep going, keep going,' he puffed out. 'Don't stop for a little thing like a nose bleed.'

The boy lowered his glove, and Millie was shocked to see

134

bright red blood on his face. His tongue came out to lick the blood as it trickled down. 'That's nothing,' Merryman panted. 'Go on.'

Millie heard her mother give a small giggle as she nervously twisted round to observe the reactions of the parents in the audience, but no one was showing signs of disapproval. 'He's only a little boy,' she whispered ambiguously to Millie.

'Guard up, move forward, punch, punch, go on.' Merryman was frantic in his exhortations to the reluctant pair, and he hopped agitatedly as they slowly lifted their gloves and cautiously stepped forward. They stood poised, one foot forward and gloves at face level, and Millie watched horrified as drops of blood fell with increasing rapidity and formed a damp mess on the floor.

Merryman puffed and grunted, squinted down at his stop-watch and suddenly blew his whistle. 'End of the round,' he called out, and grabbed the unblooded boy by the wrist. 'I declare you the winner,' he shouted, pulled the boy's arm violently upwards and beamed at the audience. There was half-hearted applause, which Millie's mother joined in, giving dainty claps and smiling benignly. Millie enjoyed clapping, and she would have joined in too, but she was distracted by Miss West who trotted into the ring with a cloth, roughly wiped the floor and then clapped the cloth onto the other boy's bloody face. She held the boy firmly by his head and walked him out of the ring, where she wrenched his gloves off him, ready for Merryman to put them on the next boy. Merryman was already tackling the other pair of gloves, and a new couple of boys were soon prepared for their bout in the ring. The audience murmured contentedly, and Millie's mother turned from side to side with a happy smile. Millie stared at the boy lying on the floor by the wall, bloodstains on his shirt and shorts, miserably dabbing his face with the cloth. The other boys were whispering and giggling, and she turned to see what Fezel was doing. But he was in conversation with Wellington, who was precluded from boxing by his spectacles. She could not judge his reaction to bleeding boys. It was possible that he might approve, or at least regard it as an unfortunate necessity, even though he did not agree with boxing.

The next two boys showed greater enthusiasm in the ring. Merryman blew his whistle and hopped and jumped, but he hardly needed to urge them on. They crouched and wheeled and punched, and he only had to say, 'that's good, that's good,' at intervals. Millie found this less interesting, and she twisted and untwisted her feet round the legs of her chair. 'Sit still, darling', her mother whispered, without relaxing her smile, and Millie tapped her heels on the legs instead. She stared at the rope a few feet in front of her, forming the boxing ring. It was an interesting piece of rope, long enough for anything you could possibly want, thick enough to be absolutely strong but not so thick that you could not tie knots in it. It would do for pulling, hanging, swinging and would be perfect for lassoes. If she had a horse, she would know where to go for the rope to tie it and ride it. In fact she must watch out to see where they put the rope at the end of the boxing match.

Merryman blew his whistle, grabbed one boy's arm, jerked it upwards and called out, 'I declare the winner.' The audience applauded enthusiastically and the boys smiled. Millie joined in the clapping this time, though she was still thinking about the rope. Had she seen it in use before? It was not thick enough for a climbing rope, though it would do for a swing. It was too thick for skipping and no use for cutting into short lengths. It would be good for a tug-of-war, which she had witnessed in action on Sports Day, and perhaps that was where she had already seen the rope.

Two more boys came into the ring, and Millie's interest revived. They were skinnier and more cringing than the first pair. Merryman flapped and gasped and raged. She noticed dribble splashing from the corner of his mouth, and he seemed to have become lumpier all over. One boy, goaded on by the exasperated Merryman, put down his head, stuck out his arms and charged blindly forward, hitting the second boy full in the stomach. Loud wails immediately came from the second boy as he doubled up, clutched himself and burst into tears.

'Out, out, out of the ring, both of you,' Merryman screamed and blew his whistle repeatedly while he waved with his arm. The two boys scrambled away, one of them sobbing wildly, and the audience tittered and applauded to cover up their embarrassment.

Two bigger boys came under the rope next and stood in the centre of the ring, squaring their shoulders and holding their gloves with confidence. Merryman smiled proudly, blew his whistle and waved his hand. 'Now, you show them how it's done,' he said, and he stood beside them without hopping. At once the boys closed in and started hitting out with firm, calculated blows, and Millie watched fascinated. One boy, slightly smaller, hit fast with both fists and the blows landed on the other's chest and shoulders. The taller boy bounced up and down and waited, and when he did punch it was with his right arm and to the head. Millie could hear the grunt when the smaller boy received a blow, and she was filled with admiration when he carried on unflinchingly.

'Up, up, keep your punches up,' Merryman advised him, with immediate effect as the smaller boy struck out and hit the other boy unexpectedly on the chin. The taller boy staggered back, startled and sore. 'Don't forget your guard,' was Merryman's advice to him, and the taller boy came back more warily with his gloves up to his face.

They circled each other cautiously, and Merryman was compelled to mutter, 'punch, punch.' The smaller boy hit out with a few ill-aimed punches, and Millie watched the taller boy as he hunched his shoulders and wriggled sideways. The flesh of his back moved in different directions, and his arms bulged with muscles just as a strong man was meant to be. Millie had not observed anatomy in action so closely before, content simply to watch the moving bodies in front of her.

At last the taller boy judged the moment right, and he gathered all his strength and lashed out with his right arm. The glove hit

137

the head in the middle of the forehead, and the smaller boy leant back, in fact it seemed to Millie that for an instant the boy actually flew, as his feet were off the ground, his head lay back and he shot horizontally towards the rope. A moment later he had crashed to the ground and lay unmoving with closed eyes.

'One,' Merryman shouted. 'Two. Three. Four. Five.' But his counting got no further as Matron had jumped up and scuttled forward to look closer at the boy. Miss West ran round the ring with the dirty cloth and knelt by him, waving the cloth in front of his face. Millie's mother twisted round, her hands fluttering. 'He didn't know his own strength,' she said with a little laugh to the row behind her. 'I'm sure it won't be serious.' The parents stared back, unsure yet how to respond, and peered at the supine boy. The English master stood up and watched, frowning, and Fezel and Wellington nudged each other.

'The winner,' Merryman called out, holding up the taller boy's arm. Then he slapped the boy on the back. 'Well done, well done. Now go and remove your gloves, one of the boys will help you.' But the boy stood staring in bewilderment at his victim.

'He's coming round,' Miss West cried out, and Matron stood up facing the audience and looked pointedly at the group of staff.

'I need two men,' she said crisply. 'The boy must be carried to the sickroom.'

'I'm coming,' the English master said, already striding to the front, and the French master followed him.

'He's always so ready to help,' Millie's mother murmured wistfully, speaking her thoughts aloud.

'Who is?' Millie said clearly, although she knew quite well who her mother was referring to.

'Oh, darling.' Her mother fluttered her hands. 'Did I say something?' She brushed her hand over Millie's hair. 'The poor boy was knocked out, but I'm sure he'll soon be better.'

'What's knocked out?' Millie asked automatically, but the conversation stopped while they watched the limp boy being lifted by the two masters and carried out of the gym, attended by Matron and Miss West.

Merryman stood in the centre of the ring and beamed nervously at the audience. 'That will be the end of the boxing contests,' he shouted, but the assorted members of the audience were already talking among themselves and forming small groups. Millie's mother stood up and surveyed the parents, ready with reassurance if needed, and Millie slipped round the rows of chairs and approached Alan from the back. He was standing up with his father, prepared to leave but having a good look round first.

'Hello, Alan,' Millie said confidently, on sure ground inside the school building. Mr. Green turned to look at her with a hard, cool stare, but he said nothing, and Alan pointed to the wall bars and the climbing ropes looped up to one side.

'That's real good stuff, I 'aven't seen such a big gym.'

'Would you like to come back?' Millie said. 'I could ask Miss West, I'm sure she'd let us.'

'Another day,' Mr. Green said non-committally, but Alan excitedly pushed past him and joined Millie behind the chairs.

'That'd be great,' Alan said, looking up to the heavy metal hooks which joined the ropes to the girder in the roof. 'I'd climb right up to the top there, you'd see, and then I'd show you some swings and jumps.'

'None of your tricks,' Mr. Green said gruffly, but Alan treated the matter as settled.

'What 'bout next week?' Alan asked. 'It's my 'Arf Term.'

'I'm not sure,' Millie said more doubtfully. 'They don't have the week off.'

'You can talk to Miss West,' Mr. Green said firmly to Millie. 'Then you can tell us what she says.' He put his hand on Alan's shoulder. 'We'll be going now.' They moved towards the door, and Millie's mother fluttered in front of them.

'It's lovely to see you at a school function, Mr. Green. I'm so glad you could come.' She put her head on one side and smiled. 'Did you enjoy the boxing, Alan?'

Alan stared up at her and said nothing, and Mr. Green shook

139

him by the shoulder. 'Yes, Mrs. Newman,' Alan muttered finally.

'It was a mixed bunch,' Mr. Green said heartily. 'Some of 'em weren't too sure what they were doing.'

Millie's mother laughed uncertainly. 'It's so difficult, boxing, isn't it?' She held out her hand to Millie while smiling at Mr. Green. 'The boys are so sweet, though, they do try hard.'

'Thank you, Mrs. Newman.' Mr. Green sounded both polite and severe, ending the conversation and walking away, guiding Alan in front of him.

'Millie darling, we must go now.' Her mother still held out her hand and smiled.

'I can't go now,' Millie said in a sudden panic. 'I've got things to do.'

'What have you got to do?' Her mother looked amused. 'Is it so very important?'

'Yes,' Millie said tensely. 'Very important things.'

'What can they be?' her mother clapped her hands as if it was a game.

'I can't tell you,' Millie said, and then at once regretted it.

'You can't tell me?' Her mother crouched down in front of her and looked straight into her eyes. 'You can't tell your own mother? Is it something so terrible?'

'Oh, no,' Millie said quickly, backing away, and then she smiled coyly. 'It's to be a secret.'

'A secret?' Her mother leant forward eagerly, her head level with Millie's. 'Oh darling, how lovely.' She clasped her hands together. 'Is it to be a surprise for me?' She stretched out her hands lovingly, placing them gently on Millie's arms, and Millie stepped back sharply, causing her mother to topple forward onto her knees with a clumsy bump and grab unceremoniously at a chair.

'Are you all right, Mrs. Newman?' Cook strode up and stood above her, large and forbidding. 'Not another accident, I hope.'

Millie's mother sat back on her heels and looked up laughing. 'It's nothing, thank you, Cook. So silly of me.' She remained sitting on the floor, leaning gracefully against the chair with one

140

arm flung out across the seat and smoothing back her loose strands of hair with her other hand. Millie was gripped by a moment of terror at the thought that her mother had broken her legs but was too brave to tell anyone.

Cook frowned at Millie and pointed to her mother. 'Millie, you can help your mother.' But Millie watched helplessly, cautious about making another move, and unsure how to approach a collapsed body. 'Give your mother a hand, Millie,' Cook repeated.

Her mother's hand fluttered in the air. 'You're not to fuss, Cook, please, I can manage.' She continued to laugh gently, leaning her head against the chair in an elegant pose, and Cook glared down in disgust at both Millie and her mother. When neither of them moved, Cook placed her hands firmly on her hips and wagged her head.

'Come on now, Mrs. Newman,' Cook said, sounding like the strictest of school-mistresses. 'Can you stand up?' Millie's mother gave a soulful sigh, and Millie stared with suspicion at her mother's legs, folded back beneath the pleats of her skirt.

'Oh darling,' Millie's mother said, smiling at Millie. 'Don't worry about me.' Millie watched her mother warily as she rested relaxed on the floor, patting back her hair and shaking her head with a demure smile. Cook shifted impatiently beside them, and Millie looked up to see Miss West return briskly round the boxing ring and call to the subdued row of boys still waiting by the wall. Most of the audience had gone, leaving untidy rows of empty chairs while Millie stood in the strange little group in the centre of the gym. Miss West beckoned to the boys and quickly marched them out before Cook could attract her attention, but the English master, re-appearing at the same time at the gym door, saw Cook stoutly waving her hand and stamping her foot among the disorderly chairs.

'What's going on?' he called out, and he pushed forward through the chairs, shoving them to each side, until he saw Millie's mother on the floor. Then he stopped and his mouth fell open, a look of horror and fear on his face. Millie had never seen such a dramatic expression appear so instantly on a face. Certainly her father would never have shown such a reaction and Millie was duly impressed.

'There,' Cook snapped disdainfully and folded her arms.

Millie's mother flung back her head and looked up over her shoulder at the English master. 'Oh, oh,' she cried, and lifted up her hands. 'There's nothing wrong, I promise you.'

The English master stepped forward and took hold of her hands. 'But what has happened?', he asked, at once forming a romantic picture.

'She must have slipped,' Cook said grimly, but the romantic scene continued.

'Help me up, please,' Millie's mother said weakly and raised herself slightly, shifting her weight onto his hands. He immediately pulled her up and grasped her with one arm round her waist. 'Oh, oh,' she said again, her hand now fluttering to her neck. 'How lucky you came along.'

'Are you all right?' he asked, looking into her face with concern.

'There,' Cook said, shaking her folded arms across her ample chest. 'I said she could stand.'

Millie's mother looked down shyly and brushed the folds of her skirt with her hand. 'Take me to the drawing room,' she whispered, but the English master still stood holding her tightly and looked at her with puzzlement. Millie stood close to the pair, unnoticed by them, and watched her mother's hand flutter up to the English master's chest and rest on his jacket lapel, which gentle reassurance, together with a brilliant smile, caused him to take her by the elbow and guide her round towards the door. Cook stood back, grunting crossly, and Millie watched the pair walk silently out of the gym.

'There was nothing wrong with your mother,' Cook exploded to Millie. 'Nothing at all. It's a disgrace.' But Millie was an unresponsive partner and Cook looked round for someone else to share her indignation. 'It's teatime,' Cook concluded, not seeing anyone suitable, and Millie guessed she would go straight

142

to the pantry and recount the tale to the Hambles. Millie at once trotted to the back of the gym, beside the piled mats and the vaulting-horse, where she was more likely to be able to hang about without being sent away and could keep an eye on the rope.

Indeed, Merryman now returned, carrying the boxing gloves and shaking his head absent-mindedly, and walked up to the post at the corner of the ring. The last of the audience, two chatting parents and a bored boy, had finally left, and the gym was now empty except for Merryman and Millie at each end, but Millie could still hear someone talking, complaining in a low voice. She looked round the gym and gradually realized that it was Merryman, talking to the post. He had not seen her. She kept very still, pressed between the mats and the side of the horse, and she watched Merryman as he shook the gloves and raised his voice. The gym had an echo, but once she had become accustomed to it, she could make out some of the words. 'No support at all,' he said, and then a jumble of angry words, ending with, 'entirely on my own.' Was he feeling weak? Millie was not keen to witness another collapse.

'Assistance,' rang out sharply, and Millie nervously drew in her breath. There were more growled words, and then, very loudly, 'a mere woman.' Could he be referring to her mother? He raised the gloves in the air, and snarled out, 'they give me a woman assistant,' and flung down the gloves. It became clear that he was talking about Miss West, and Millie immediately felt sorry for her. She had done nothing to deserve such a tirade.

However, it seemed to have calmed him, and he picked up the gloves and started walking straight towards Millie's corner of the gym. Would he pick on her next? She squeezed herself against the horse, and he stopped abruptly and looked up.

'Who's that?' he said sharply.

Millie decided instinctively that attack was the best defence. 'Boo, Mr. Merryman,' she called out, leaning round the side of the horse. 'I'm playing sardines.'

'Sar-dines?' Merryman drawled the word in amazement. Then

143

he quickly looked round the gym. 'Who with? Who are you playing with?'

Millie laughed. 'With myself. I'm used to playing on my own.'

Merryman stared at her. 'But you can't play sardines by yourself,' he said suspiciously.

'I can.' She jumped towards him, both feet together in a distracting movement. 'I can. I hide, and then I look.' She knew this would be difficult to explain. 'I have to pretend I don't know where I'm hiding.' This was not helping, and more distraction was needed. 'Where do you keep the gloves?' she said gaily and skipped the last stretch up to him.

Merryman looked down at her with distaste. 'Why do you want to know?' he said crossly, and then he relaxed a little. 'Do you want to hide in the glove box then?' He gave a short laugh. 'No one would find you in there.' He waved his hand towards the row of wooden boxes attached to the wall at the end of the gym. The boys used them as a platform, to sit and stand on, and the lids could be lifted up to reveal balls, bats, rings, netting and all kinds of gymnastic aids. Two of the boxes had padlocks, and Millie was curious to see which one he used for the gloves. She was not surprised when he went to the middle box with the heavy padlock and pulled vainly at the lid.

'What a nuisance,' he muttered, and rattled the lock. 'Who shut it?' He stood up with a sigh and fumbled in his trouser pocket.

'I've got the key, Mr. Merryman,' Miss West called out from the other end of the gym. Neither Millie nor Merryman had heard her come in, and they both jumped round in surprise. She came towards them, smiling and holding up a small key on the end of a ribbon. 'Here it is, don't worry.'

'Er, thank you Miss West, er, thank you,' Merryman mumbled in confusion, and Millie stared at his cheeks which shook and wobbled just as his knees had done.

Miss West ran lightly between the chairs and up to the end of the gym. 'I'll finish clearing up, don't worry.' She swung the little key and he automatically held out his large flabby hand. 'You do

144

the gloves,' she said laughing and dropped the key into his hand. 'I'll do the rest of the things. Millie, you can help.' She swung round, smiling at Millie. 'I'm glad to see you here, Millie. I tell you what, we'll put away the chairs very quickly, and then there'll be time to show you the ropes.'

'The ropes?' Millie was filled with excitement, and for once was compelled to jump and clap. 'Oh yes, please.' But then she stopped, confused as to which ropes she meant. However, there was no opportunity to stand and reflect as Miss West had already run back to the chairs.

'Come on, Millie, to work. You push the chairs up to my end.' Miss West bustled at one side of the gym, stacking one chair on top of another with a loud clatter. Millie grasped the side of a chair and found it easy to run across the gym pushing the chair in front of her.

'Don't do that,' Merryman shrieked from the far end of the gym, and Millie stopped still, resting on the chair. 'Don't do that,' he repeated more quietly. 'You'll mark the floor.'

'Don't worry about that,' Miss West shouted, almost angrily. 'The floor's marked enough as it is.' Millie started pushing again and left the chair beside Miss West while she went to fetch another one.

'There's no respect these days,' Merryman said, shaking all over as he walked down to Miss West. 'No wonder the place is deteriorating.' She continued to clatter the chairs together, and Millie pushed up the next one. 'How can you teach the boys respect,' he went on plaintively, 'when they see such careless behaviour.'

'Don't fuss so,' Miss West said sharply. 'Thank you, Millie,' she added as Millie left another chair beside her.

'There's no example set for the boys,' he muttered, walking away. 'They think they can do as they like. That's no way to run a school, I never dreamed I would see such lack of discipline, what a pretty mess we've come to.'

'Faster, Millie, faster,' Miss West shouted cheerfully. Millie was having to move further away to bring the chairs to the growing piles. She chased empty-handed across the gym and ran back noisily with a chair. The harder she pushed, the more it squeaked on the floor, and she giggled as she ran.

'Enough of that, Millie, work is a serious matter,' Miss West said, though she was half smiling herself. Millie giggled the more, and Miss West suddenly stopped, frowning crossly.

'Don't forget to take down the boxing ring,' Merryman called out from the door.

'Don't worry, Mr. Merryman,' Miss West said as he left, and then she turned to Millie. 'Now get on with the work. We want to get it finished quickly.' She briskly set to with the chairs again, and Millie concentrated on bringing up the rest of the chairs with efficient speed.

'Excellent,' Miss West said triumphantly when all the chairs were stacked. 'Well done Millie. Now we must coil the rope.' She ran down to one corner of the boxing ring, pulled out the post and laid it on the floor. Millie ran down after her and started tugging at the rope.

'Don't do that,' Miss West shouted, just as Merryman had done, and Millie stopped again. 'We've got to take the posts out first,' she said, moving to the next corner. Millie waited while all four posts were laid down, and Miss West unhooked the two ends of the rope. 'Now pull,' Miss West ordered, and Millie slowly drew in the rope, hand over hand, until half of it lay in an untidy pile at her feet.

'Oh my goodness,' Miss West said, when she saw the results of Millie's efforts. 'Not like that.' She was walking round the ring, gathering the posts together. 'Wait a minute, and I'll show you how to coil it.' Millie stood obediently by the rope while Miss West returned the posts to the correct box at the far end of the gym.

'Now,' Miss West said, coming back. 'Find one end.' Millie inspected the rope and picked up the end carefully.

'What can you use this rope for?' Millie asked, shaking the end so that it wagged up and down.

'Making a boxing ring,' Miss West said, laughing. 'Or

anything else you like.'

'Can you tie knots with it?' Millie went on. 'Could you make a lasso?'

'Yes, of course,' Miss West said impatiently.

'Will you show me?' Millie said quickly.

'Don't waste my time.' Miss West became suddenly cross again. 'Place the end on the floor. Go on. We're going to coil it.' Millie dropped the end of the rope, neatly bound with string and with a hook attached, down in front of her and looked up, waiting. 'Now lay the rope round in a circle on the floor.' Miss West stood a short distance away, her feet in white gym shoes placed firmly apart, her white shirt and shorts glittering with cleanliness to indicate her efficiency, and gave her orders. 'Take the rope and turn it as you lay it down.' Millie held the rope near the end and moved it in a circle close to the floor, but the end whipped round after her. Miss West laughed, but did not move to help her. 'You must hold the end down to begin with.' Millie put her hand flat on the rope, but then she found she could not turn the rope with her one free hand, so she stamped fiercely on the rope with her foot, and Miss West laughed again as she watched. Millie pulled the rope to lie before her foot, and soon an uneven circle formed on the floor. 'You must shake the rope before you put it down,' Miss West went on. 'So that it stays flat.' Millie felt the rope in her hands as she twisted and shook it, and sometimes it turned as she wanted and sometimes it seemed to have a life of its own and then it kicked in the opposite direction. She enjoyed giving it an extra firm twist and making it form a proper circle.

'Carry on,' Miss West said, and she walked away up the empty gym. Millie struggled with the rope, the coils increasing on the floor, until she heard a piercing squeak and, looking up, she saw that Miss West had released another rope, a long thin one, from its hook on the wall, and it squeaked and rattled through the pulley in the ceiling, letting the thick climbing ropes come thumping down.

'Ooh, lovely,' Millie cried out, and was startled to hear her voice echo round the gym.

'Finish that first,' Miss West shouted as she freed the thick ropes, and Millie worked hard, the circles becoming increasingly irregular, until the other end jerked on to the pile.

'I've done it,' Millie shouted and waved her arms.

Miss West swung gently against the climbing rope, holding it with her arm high above her head. 'Now pick up the coil,' she shouted back, and Millie looked down at the mass of rope at her feet. 'Put one hand underneath,' Miss West shouted. 'Right to the centre. Then the other hand on top, and hold hands. Carry it like a big ring.'

Millie bent down and wriggled her hand under the rough rope. Her chin touched the top of the pile, and the rope smelt dusty. Just then she hated the whole length of the rope and all its malevolent twists and turns. She clasped her hands as directed, and tried to stand up, but the rope was much heavier than she had expected, and she fell forward on top of it.

Miss West's loud laugh echoed round the gym. 'And again,' she shouted heartily. 'Don't give up. Try again.'

Millie staggered to her feet and heaved up the coils of rope, clutching them against her dress and took small steps across the gym.

'That's right,' Miss West sung out, and pushing away her thick rope to leave it slowly swinging, she walked leisurely to the end box and lifted the lid. 'It goes in here,' she shouted, holding open the lid, but she had to wait some time while Millie shuffled across the whole length of the gym. 'You see what you can do if you try,' Miss West said as Millie reached the box. 'Now put it away in here.'

Millie leant over the edge of the box and unclasped her hands, letting the coils thump down and stretched her stiff arms with relief. 'Not like that, oh, not like that,' Miss West cried. 'It's all undone again.' Millie stared miserably into the box, and Miss West relented.

'It doesn't matter,' she said, patting Millie on the head, and she let the lid drop down with a crash, causing Millie to jump and

148

shudder. Miss West gave her loud laugh and ran back to the swinging rope.

'Hooray,' she shouted, as if she had become a child. 'Now we can do some climbing.' She grasped the rope with her hands above and her ankles below, and flung back her head with abandon. 'Aaah,' she called out, swinging slightly on the rope.

Millie ignored her and looked at the closed box where the rope was kept. There was no place for a padlock, so it was left unlocked, and it was easy to identify, being the one at the end. She felt reassured, in case she should ever need the rope, and she also knew that she could carry it by herself, if necessary. She smiled with secret contentment and turned to look at Miss West, who was swinging higher backwards and forwards.

'Aaaahh,' Miss West said dreamily, as if to herself, and Millie walked slowly towards her until she was near enough to feel the brush of air as the white form swung past. 'Whoops,' Miss West shouted suddenly, and, letting go of the rope, she jumped down to the floor, landing neatly with bent knees. 'Now it's your turn,' she said, standing erect and holding out her arms to Millie.

Millie's two hands, when she placed them each side of the thick rope, hardly met at the thumbs and fingers. She looked despairingly to the ceiling, and the rope seemed longer than ever. Miss West dropped to her knees beside Millie and held the rope near the bottom.

'Stand on my hands,' she said. 'Hold on tight.' Millie stepped up onto Miss West's fists and embraced the rope and suddenly found that she was free of the floor and it was easy after all to climb a rope.

'Hold on, hold on,' Miss West said excitedly, and she quickly took away her hands and placed them higher up. Millie scrambled for a new footing and slid her hands up. She was climbing a rope.

Miss West repeated her hand-hold until Millie was higher than the level of her head. Millie hugged the rope and did not risk the movement to look down. 'Now slide down,' Miss West said. 'Put one hand down first, and then the other.' She stepped away from the rope, removing her hands, but Millie could not hold on unsupported, and she slid with a rapid crash to the floor. The rough rope had rubbed her arms and legs, and she sat miserably beneath it, feeling sore in many places.

'You'll soon learn,' Miss West said brightly. 'There's no permanent harm done.' Millie remained on the floor and inspected her knees and her elbows, while Miss West ran to the side and took the thin rope from the hook, coming back to loop it round the climbing rope above Millie.

'Up you get now,' Miss West said, and she pulled at the rope, making it squeak through the pulley again. The climbing ropes jerked up, and Millie watched as they rose to their high loops by the ceiling. She still sat on the empty gym floor, watching Miss West as she moved with neat white efficiency, attaching the thin rope to its hook and leaving all in order.

Miss West laughed loudly, so that it echoed round the gym and, bounding forward, she grabbed Millie's arms, pulling her to her feet. She held Millie by the wrist and gave a great leaping skip, lifting Millie up with her, and Millie was forced to skip too, with flying jumps, and they crossed the gym together, leaping and skipping, Miss West's white gym shoes flashing energetically and Millie pulled up into the air at each bound.

'Wasn't that fun,' Miss West said, laughing at Millie, and Millie smiled back uncertainly as they ran out of the gym hand in hand.

11

Millie stood beside her father in front of the cricket pavilion, listening idly as he discussed the state of the pitch with Mr. Green. On the next Saturday was the School match against the Old Boys, and her father must ensure that all aspects of the school were seen at their best. There had been rain the day before, and they were deciding whether to leave the mowing of the grass until the following afternoon.

Millie was sure that Miss Ellen had been talking to her father, because after lunch he had questioned her about her reading, and then he had taken her with him everywhere he went, to the Art room where he looked briefly round the walls, to the pantry where he had an unusually serious conversation with Hamble, then quickly into the Junior Library, where he muttered crossly to himself, and then to the masters' common room, where he had a noisy talk with the English master. Then they had walked briskly and silently along the path by the football field, to end up at the swimming pond where her father spoke for a long time with Merryman, standing on the wooden duck-boards at the edge of the water. Millie stood well back, on the path to the changing hut, not wishing to be splashed by the boys excitedly jumping into the water while unsupervised, and she warily examined the surrounding grass for stray frogs. But no frogs appeared, and all she found was an empty cigarette packet. She showed this to her father when he had finished talking to Merryman, and she was surprised by the vehemence of his angry reaction. She knew he sometimes could be unexpectedly cross, but this seemed to throw him into a disproportionate rage. All the way back along the path he lectured her on the evils of deceitful behaviour and on the terrible consequences of doing secret acts behind the backs of those in charge who were only trying to do their best. Miss Ellen must surely have said something to him.

But what could she have said? Admittedly Millie had been completely fed up that morning and had been as difficult as she could be, but she had been careful not to give away any secrets. It had started when she asked Miss Ellen if she was a Jew, and Miss Ellen had told her not to be cheeky, and Millie had been knowingly rude, calling Miss Ellen a bloody nitwit, a phrase she had picked up from Wellington. Miss Ellen had ordered her to write out lines, a rare punishment, and Millie had swept everything on the table onto the floor, books, papers, Miss Ellen's knitting, a cup and saucer, pens, crayons and drawing books, secure in the knowledge that they could give her orders, shut her in her room, deprive her of food, beat her, threaten her, shout at her, but they could not touch her. She was ultimately all-powerful.

Miss Ellen had shouted remorselessly, screaming angry insults at Millie, and then let slip that the local girls' school would not take her, she had such a bad reputation. Millie felt a sharp frisson as she realized that her fame was much wider than she had previously believed. She now had an image to keep up, and this gave her food for thought as she absent-mindedly picked up a book and returned it to the table. But Miss Ellen knew nothing of her Grand Master Plan, she was sure, so it could only have been trivial matters that she had passed on to her father.

The mowing of the grass was settled at last, and her father and Mr. Green contentedly surveyed the expanse of fresh green grass, as if the job was already done. Suddenly Mr. Green looked at Millie.

'There is a proper place for everyone,' he said, and Millie waited, uncertain whether he was speaking to her, or even about her.

'Some may be a bad influence,' he went on, still looking firmly at her, and she began to feel uncomfortable, though it was not clear what he was referring to.

152

'Inside the house, that's your business,' he said, frowning at Millie. Then he blurted out, 'it'd be best if you kept away from Taverner.'

'I'm sure Taverner wouldn't cause any trouble,' her father said quickly. 'He would never make untoward suggestions.'

'That is your opinion,' Mr. Green said ponderously. 'And it is my opinion.' He looked backwards and forwards from Millie to her father. 'Have you asked her?'

'Of course, that would be my concern, and mine only,' her father said uncomfortably. His hands were in his pockets, but the coins were silent. 'And the rest of the garden is all right?' he added mildly.

'Yes, yes.' Mr. Green looked towards the distant walled garden. 'It's coming along nicely.' He paused thoughtfully. 'I leave it to you then.' He gave a final stare at Millie, though he was clearly talking to her father.

'Yes, we must be going too,' her father said, though Mr. Green had not moved, and he raised his hand in a general acknowledgement and nodded. 'Come along, Millie.' Her father sounded particularly austere, and he looked round and about and straightened his shoulders in a most Headmasterly manner. Millie kept pace with his even walk as he started back round the edge of the cricket field, skirting the thick grove of bamboos said to be only fit for monkeys, and Mr. Green, having had his say, returned to the pavilion and was soon out of earshot.

'I think it would be best,' her father said eventually, speaking slowly and gravely, 'if you saw no more of the Green boy.'

'What?' Millie said immediately. Surprises would never cease, as there had been no mention of his boy from Mr. Green. 'D'you mean Alan?' She would, for the moment, stand by her friend.

'Ah, yes, Alan.' Her father kept on at his steady pace, frowning at the ground in front of him. 'Yes. You should no longer play with him.'

'Why?' Millie said, perplexed and indignant. 'Why?'

Her father flapped his elbows, keeping his hands in his trouser pockets. 'He is not suitable for you.' He lifted his head

153

importantly. 'You must understand that there are some people with whom it is not correct for you to associate.'

'Why?' Millie repeated, as, not for the first time, nothing was any clearer.

'You cannot mix with him,' her father said gruffly. 'In any case, it only leads to trouble.'

'Don't know what you mean,' Millie muttered, but her father did not reply. She was not sure whether he was speaking in general moral terms or at last referring to the Spontaneous Rehearsal in the walled garden. She did not want to press him too far, but she needed some clarification. 'Can I talk to him, then?'

'As I have said,' her father replied with a note of irritation, 'I would prefer you not to have Alan as your companion.'

Millie pouted her lips, filled with rage at the total unreasonableness of life. Then she spoke bitterly. 'I was with Alan in the gym. Can I do that? Can I be with Fezel? Can I mix with him?'

Her father looked round vaguely. 'You will find that there are some circumstances in which it is perfectly acceptable to meet people for the purpose of conversation or to carry out work together, for instance.' Millie was forcefully reminded of Miss Ellen's 'there is a time and a place for everything,' a phrase which she used frequently to lay down rules for her convenience. 'There are other circumstances to be avoided, as they may lead to misunderstanding, or worse, to criminal activity.' He gave Millie a sidelong glance. 'A close association with one other person is always open to danger and such friendships are prone to result in calamity.' He attempted a reassuring smile. 'I am saying that you are not to go off for long stretches of time on your own with your particular friend. It is unseemly, and unsafe.'

Millie took a deep breath. 'Do you mean that with anyone?'

Her father managed a more expansive smile. 'It would be preferable if you chose your friends with caution.' He tilted his head and jingled a coin in his pocket. 'You have your parents for guidance.'

154

'I mean,' Millie persisted, 'do you mean that not anyone must have a friend?'

Her father wagged his head with amusement. 'We are all subject to the same laws, whether we like it or not, and you will learn, as you grow older, to choose your friends wisely.'

'What about the English master?' Millie said abruptly.

Her father's amused mood disappeared at once. 'What about him?' he asked crisply.

'My mother,' she spat out the words, 'is his friend, I know, because they had breakfast on the bedroom balcony, just the two of them in the holidays, and they're still friends, I know, because . . .'

'That's enough,' her father interrupted. His elbows and shoulders tensed, and his walk became curiously stiff while keeping the same regular pace. 'I don't want to hear any lies,' he said clearly.

'It's not lies,' Millie cried indignantly, stamping along beside him. 'Miss Ellen knows.'

They had reached the front lawn, treading on the soft grass which usually gave off a warm dank smell. Now it was as if they were suddenly surrounded by chill air, cutting out all sounds and smells, and they were frozen in a strange stiff world, where all the ominous stabs and deadly thunderbolts were held immobile. The pair walked on, bound in icy silence, and Millie for a moment almost enjoyed the protection from common existence, freeing her from troubling humanity.

But she knew it would not last, and the crunch of their feet on the gravel drive broke the spell. Her father raised his arm towards the front door.

'I have work to do now indoors. You may play for the next hour on your own, but I do not wish you to go out of sight of the house. Nor do I wish you to bring me tales of others, whether they are true or false.' He spoke in his quiet, even voice, the sonorous tones accentuating the air of stern purposefulness. But he seemed too tired to stamp his personality, and he walked to the door without looking round.

155

Millie ran, without waiting, as fast as she could, down the drive, past the new wing, past the kitchen yard, past the gym entrance, past the sheds and outhouses, until she reached the first big chestnut tree of the avenue, where she stopped to catch her breath. She did not care who saw her, as all her movements already seemed to have been mapped and checked, and she looked round defiantly. But there was no one in sight, so she dropped her truculence to save her breath and continued down the grass edge of the long drive, jogging rather than running as the ground was rough. When she reached the Lodge she by-passed the front door and went directly to the wooden gate at the side of the house, which she knew led into the back yard. She opened the gate with care and meticulously closed it behind her, before looking round to see who was there.

'Hello Mrs. Green,' she called out boldly, when she found there was no one in the yard.

'Hello, who's that?' Mrs. Green's friendly voice came from the kitchen.

'It's me, Millie Newman,' Millie shouted back, and she went up to the kitchen door. 'Can I see Alan?'

Mrs. Green came to the door, smiling. 'Alan's in his shed. You go and talk to him. I'm busy now.' She quickly disappeared indoors, and Millie crossed the yard to the open shed where Alan kept his boxes. At first she could not see him, but on peering in she saw him stirring on the ground at the far corner of the shed.

'What are you doing?' Millie asked in astonishment.

'Plannin' an attack.' He crawled out backwards from behind a carefully arranged pile of boards and straw. 'That's the secret landin' strip, in there. Them planes's hidden, all camflarged.' Millie watched, disappointed. 'Then over 'ere,' Alan said, proudly pointing to a row of toy aeroplanes on a large sheet of cardboard. 'These're the ones ready to take off.' Millie looked at the detailed drawings of the runways on the cardboard. He had even added pictures of coloured lights at the end, and he had constructed a rough square cardboard building at one side, presumably to represent a shed. 'There's the control tower, see?'

156

Alan said, indicating the shed-like structure. 'They're all ready, waitin' for the go-a'ead.' Millie sighed. Such care and hard work, and to what purpose? She had bigger plans to think of.

'I can't stay long,' she said, but she remained by the cardboard runway, not wishing to upset Alan as he was part of the plan.

'You can 'elp fly the planes, if yer like,' he said tentatively.

'No, I couldn't do that,' she said hurriedly. 'I mean,' she added, 'I don't have time.'

'You could stay a bit,' he said casually.

'I came to invite you to play on the ropes. You remember the ropes?' Millie paused, hoping she would not have to explain too much.

Alan looked at her thoughtfully. 'You mean, them ropes in the gym?'

'That's right,' Millie said, relieved. 'You said you wanted to swing on them. Well, I've arranged it.'

'Cor,' Alan said, clearly excited by the news. 'That's great. When d'I come up to the gym?'

'They're set up outside now,' Millie said, using her grand voice to indicate superior knowledge. 'For a special treat.'

'Outside?' Alan said doubtfully. 'Where?'

'I'll show you,' Millie said even more grandly. 'They'll be ready on Saturday.'

'Saturday?' Alan repeated.

'That's right,' Millie said authoritatively. 'You come up to . . .' She paused, suitable meeting places running through her mind.

'To the gym?' Alan asked.

'No, no,' Millie shouted fiercely. 'You must not come to the gym.' Her face screwed up like an attacking animal.

'Orl right orl right,' Alan said indignantly. 'Keep yer 'air on.'

Millie glowered at him. 'We must meet somewhere else.' Her words came out grimly.

'Where d'we meet, then?' Alan said reasonably.

She paused again, and then in her mind's eye she saw the perfect place. 'Behind the cricket pavilion,' she shouted delightedly, and she beamed at Alan.

157

'On a Saturday?' He gaped at her. 'I'm not allowed.' His voice rose in horror. 'I couldn't do that. There'll be a match on.'

'Yes, you can,' Millie said angrily. 'You can say something, can't you? Say you're looking for your father.'

Alan frowned. 'But 'e wouldn't be there on a Saturday.'

'Say something else then,' Millie replied crossly. 'Anyway, there'll be so many people there going in and out and watching and so on that nobody will notice you.' She spoke knowingly, from her own experience.

Alan still looked nervous. 'But why that place? Seems a silly place ter me.'

'It's a very good place.' Millie stamped out the words. 'That's where everyone will be, so it's the best place to meet.' She smiled slyly. 'And it's the nearest to the ropes, too.'

'Is that where the ropes 'll be?' Alan said, surprised.

'Somewhere round there,' Millie said very grandly. 'I'll take you to them, on Saturday.'

'Orl right then,' Alan said hesitantly.

'It'll be great fun,' Millie stated decisively. 'I'll be there, anyway.' She spoke more gently. 'I'll wait for you.'

'What time?' Alan ostentatiously looked at the large new watch on his wrist.

'Three o'clock,' Millie said quickly. She knew that the cricket match would be under way by then.

Alan suddenly laughed. 'S'funny idea.'

Millie would not be drawn from her serious demeanour. 'I'll have it all arranged. I'll meet you there on Saturday.' She stepped backwards into the yard, keeping her eye on Alan as if this would prevent him from changing his mind.

'Yea, I'll be there,' he said, still giggling as he watched her crossing the yard.

Millie made sure that the yard gate was properly closed behind her, as she did not want any irrelevant trouble from her visit there. She felt contented as she pondered on her plans, because she liked action when it came and she found it pleasantly stimulating. What else did she have to do before Saturday? She

158

counted off on her fingers her different tasks, as she slowly walked back up the drive. There was the rope to get, out of the box in the gym, and dragged all the way up to the rhododendron bushes in the grove. This had to be timed carefully, and a perfect moment, she realized, was after her tea, when she was supposed to be preparing for bed and all the boys and the staff were concentrated in the dining room for their supper. She could pass round the back of the building and there would be no one in the classrooms to look out for her, and she could cross outside the empty Gallery room with impunity and reach the safe thickets of the grove by the back end. She had decided to attempt the arduous trek herself, because she already had much to ask of the boys, and she did not want to risk stretching their willingness too far. She must ask Fezel to supervise the knots, and he would need help in lifting the ropes into the trees, and she would approach her faithful Wellington for this. Then she must find a box to stand on, and perhaps some more string or handkerchieves, and she was sure that more support would be needed and she would get Draper in for this, as he would surely do as he was told. She shivered, appalled at the amount of arranging to be done in the short time before Saturday. But it must be completed, or the plans would fail and the opportunity would be lost. She strode forward, her fists clenched, her lips held firm, and her will set on course with inflexible determination.

12

The Old Boys, gathered in front of the cricket pavilion for their annual match, were of all ages and aptitudes, from cocky young men who had only been away from school a year to grey-haired elders who had seen it all before. They held in common an attachment to their schooldays, and they behaved like schoolboys, or their memories of them, chaffing each other and reviving nicknames and established jokes. The actual schoolboys, on these occasions, were watchful and subdued, and determined to win the cricket match, though whether they did or not depended on the brilliance of their current players. They had certainly selected their best team possible, and they were all properly clad in white, from their heavy boots to their non-obligatory sun-hats. The Old Boys had not succeeded in presenting themselves entirely in white. Some of them had made do with white shirts and grey trousers, which they compensated for with louder jokes. These were the ones who clustered round Merryman, which contributed to him being in his element. This was Merryman's happiest day, and he beamed and bounced and slapped old shoulders, talking fast before the serious business of the match began. He was by tradition the Umpire, and the frivolities must come before and after the match, for during the match he worked hard at being seen to be fair.

Millie's father was also joyful, greeting old faces with special pleasure now that he was no longer responsible for them. He made a particular point, however, of joking with the school team, as he considered it his duty to keep up their morale. He played for the school, attaching importance to their performance on the field, and he was proud of the fact that he handed over the captaincy to the head boy and played as one of the team, thus demonstratively putting the school before himself. He was also aware of the attention of the ladies, who thronged among the players beside the pavilion. The Old Boys were encouraged to bring guests, and there were more admiring ladies present than there were players. The masters also took the opportunity to invite their lady friends, as they could relax in deck chairs at the edge of the field and afterwards there was a good supply of tea and buns.

Millie's mother moved among the ladies with extreme elegance, her hair controlled by a wide-brimmed straw hat profusely covered with artificial flowers. She enjoyed seeing familiar faces again, and she was kept busy giving her sweet welcome to every individual guest. As Millie passed near her mother, checking on her whereabouts, she heard the English master introduce her mother to his sister. Millie eyed with curiosity the gauche young woman in a pink trouser suit, as it was unusual to have a sister referred to in the school, and it was noteworthy to see one in the flesh, holding out a chubby hand while Millie's mother leant forward with an extra gushing welcome.

Millie weaved unobtrusively through the crowd, checking on everyone's position. Her father was fully occupied talking once more about the batting order with the Head Boy. All the prefects were in the team, and the senior boys who were not in the team still hung round them with encouraging remarks. Miss West was cheerfully testing the size of a much-used pair of cricket pads with an Old Boy, and Merryman drew attention to himself by shouting that it was time for the toss. It was a good moment to disappear behind the pavilion.

Millie was at once struck by the overwhelming smell of damply rotten mown grass, enclosed in the narrow stretch between the back of the pavilion and the thick bamboo. At first she could only see huge piles of grass cuttings, the nearer one still freshly green and the further ones turning brown and putrid. Then she heard muttered voices and the three boys appeared from between the piles of cut grass.

161

'You're late, you're late,' Fezel said urgently.

'You're very late,' Wellington emphasized crossly.

'We want to see the match,' Draper added.

'You said we'd be finished before the match started,' Fezel said.

'And it stinks here,' Wellington said, giggling.

'Pooh,' Draper said, and held his nose.

Millie sensed that an air of confidence was needed to deal with a rebellion. 'Come on. We'll be as quick as we can,' she said, frowning at the boys. 'Did you find a box?' she added sternly.

'What do we want a box for?' Wellington asked.

'To stand on,' Millie said briefly, looking round. 'This'll do.' She pulled at the large metal scoop used to collect the grass cuttings on the motor mower.

'You can't stand on that,' Fezel said in disgust.

'Yes you can,' Millie said. 'On its side.' She tugged it forward and rolled it over, giving it a push while the boys looked on.

'It'll wobble,' Wellington said. 'Draper, you try it.'

Draper climbed up with difficulty onto the rusty metal box, and stood up precariously. 'Yippee,' he called out and waved his arms.

'Quiet,' Millie barked. 'It'll do. Come on.'

Draper jumped down, landing in a pile of old grass. 'Aagh. Poohwee. Eerr,' he groaned, making noises as he flapped about, brushing off the sticky grass.

Millie was already at the narrow opening in the bamboo. 'Will the box get through here?' she said anxiously.

Fezel stepped forward impatiently. 'Let's get it over with,' he said, grabbing the metal box and pulling it roughly towards the bamboo. Millie lowered her head to guard against any bamboo fronds and pushed in to the crackly thicket, and Fezel noisily followed, breaking bamboo stalks as he pulled the box behind him. Millie was glad of the noise, as she could hear cheering from the other side of the pavilion and she knew that one team would have won the toss and chosen the side to bat first, and she wished to distract her confederates. She pushed at the bamboo to make it rustle, hoping that Wellington and Draper, following behind Fezel, would not be diverted by the cheers. But the three boys continued in silence, and Millie led the way with increasing confidence.

They scrambled through the bamboo and then between the dark rhododendron bushes, Millie crouching under the low branches with the boys puffing and muttering behind her, until they reached a paltry clearing round a half-grown oak tree. Here the ropes were already hanging from a branch of the tree, set up with a struggle the previous day under Millie's direction. Fezel pulled the box up to the tree and left it with a final kick, striking a hollow note as the metal reverberated.

'It'll make a drum,' Draper said excitedly, picking up a stick.

'No, no,. please, no,' Millie gasped, jumping between Draper and the metal box. Having got this far, she did not want them to be discovered prematurely by the wild beatings of a drum. She could just hear the knock of the cricket ball on the bat, and she now wished she had chosen a more remote clearing, although she knew it would have been difficult to persuade the boys to venture further into the intractable grove.

'Let's test the ropes,' Wellington said, looking up at the three long ropes hanging loosely from the tree, each one ending in an intricate knot. He raised his arms above his head and grasped the middle rope above the large ball-like knot. 'They may have slipped overnight.'

'They can't slip,' Fezel said firmly. 'They're fixed really tight.'

Wellington kicked his feet free of the ground and swung gently to and fro. 'Why did you make them so high?' he said, giggling from between his up-stretched arms. 'This one would be much better if you could sit on it.'

'That's why I brought the box,' Millie said crisply. 'To get up on.'

'It's still not high enough,' Wellington said, squinting down as he swung higher with a kick to the ground.

'You could jump up from it,' Millie said with less assurance.

'There's no need,' Fezel said, taking hold of the rope nearest

163

the tree, which was thinner than the other two and ended in a loop and a bulky twisted knob. He was taller than the other two boys and could reach the rope without stretching.

Draper, the smallest, ran towards the furthest rope and jumped up at its neat loop. 'Don't touch that,' Fezel called out, and Draper at once stood still, looking questioningly at Fezel, with the rope, which he had knocked, swinging just above his head. 'It's a lasso,' Fezel explained. 'It will tighten if you pull it.' Fezel put his hand proudly on the knot in his rope. 'I don't want them to spoil before they've been inspected.'

Wellington jumped down from the middle rope. 'This knot won't spoil,' he said confidently. 'It's rock solid.' He grabbed the rope and held it still. 'Here you are, Draper. You can have a swing on this one. I'll help you up.'

'Why not try the box,' Millie said, and she started dragging it to the centre of the clearing.

'When are these people supposed to be coming?' Fezel said crossly. 'I want to get this inspection over.'

'Yes,' Wellington said. 'I wish they'd hurry up.' He let go of the rope. 'How on earth are they going to find their way here?'

'I've got to fetch them,' Millie said tensely.

'When?' Fezel said. 'I can't wait much longer.'

'Three o'clock,' Millie said, suddenly intensely nervous.

Fezel looked at his watch. 'It's three o'clock now,' he said succinctly.

Millie jumped away from the box and rubbed her hands down the sides of her dress. 'I'll fetch them, I'll go now.' She looked at the three boys. 'You look after the ropes.' She shook her head so that her curly plaits fell behind and thrust her hands into her bulging pockets. 'I won't be long.' She stood rooted to the ground, staring at the boys.

Wellington sniggered. 'Well, go on then.'

'Hurry up,' Fezel sneered. 'Nothing will happen to the ropes.'

'We won't budge from here,' Draper said cheerfully.

'But you'd better be quick,' Wellington said with a note of warning.

Millie took a deep breath and rushed into the rhododendron bushes, beating at the branches which caught at her hair and her dress, crashing relentlessly forward until she came to the barrier of bamboo. Then she paused, alert for all sounds, and crept on, peering out at the back of the pavilion. But there was no one there in the dark and smelly space, not even between the piles of rotting grass. The boards of the pavilion were shaking from a series of shattering thumps coming from inside, and to Millie this meant that the boys waiting to bat were becoming restless and were swiping at each other. It followed, then, that all the Old Boys would be out on the field, and the numerous delighted cries of 'Howzat' indicated that her father was already batting, which placed him well away from the pavilion. Millie looked up and down, gulping back sobs of frustration at another good opportunity slipping by, and clenched her teeth while she listened to applause from the front of the pavilion and desultory cries of 'well played.' She would wait in her fusty corner for ever, even if no one turned up.

But then, suddenly, without her seeing him coming, Alan was before her. He was uncharacteristically well dressed, with a jacket and tie and polished shoes, and his hair was brushed down.

He scowled at Millie. 'Me Dad'll give me 'ell if 'e finds out I'm 'ere.' Millie quickly held his arm. 'And I mustn't get me best clothes dirty, I'm goin' out with me Dad after.'

'We'll hurry,' Millie said breathlessly. She concentrated all her energies, spider-like, on Alan, and pulled him gently by his arm towards the gap in the bamboo.

But he resisted. 'I can't play on the ropes today. I came to ask if they'd be there another day.'

'Never mind.' Millie, smiling, still pulled him by the arm. 'Just come and see them.' Her enthusiasm was appealing and he went with her through the bamboo. 'You can join the Club, anyway.'

'The Club?' Alan asked. They stopped between the bamboo and the rhododendron bushes.

'Yes,' Millie said. 'You have to join a Club to play on the ropes.'

165

'You didn't tell me that,' Alan said doubtfully.

'It's just been made,' Millie said, smiling all the time. 'And I'm here to take you to the Club.'

'What sort of a Club?' Alan asked.

'It's a special club made by the boys,' Millie's powers of improvisation reached brilliant heights in moments of tension. 'Not many people can join.'

'Can I join?' Alan said, surprised.

'They said you could join.' She nodded. 'They voted.' She remembered talk of the prefects choosing a dinner monitor. 'You got the most votes.'

'Did I?' Alan smiled proudly.

'Yes,' Millie said. 'But you have to do the rules.'

'Oh,' Alan groaned. 'What're the rules.'

'When I take you . . .' She paused, and gently holding his wrist, she moved behind him, taking his other wrist and bringing his hands together behind his back.

'What's all this,' Alan said, giggling.

'I have to tie your hands behind your back.' She quickly pulled string out of her pocket and started winding it round his wrists.

'Don't be silly,' Alan said, looking round and pulling away his hands.

'Really,' Millie said, nodding and smiling. 'Honest. Let me finish. I can't take you if they aren't tied.'

'I've never 'eard anythin' so silly,' he said, but he held his hands still while she wound the string round and pulled the ends tight.

'Ow,' Alan said. 'Not really tight.'

'It's all right,' Millie said, holding him by his arm. 'I haven't made a real knot.'

Alan wriggled his hands. 'You've made it too tight.'

'No, I haven't.' Millie was impatient now. 'Come on. They won't wait much longer.' She gripped his arm tight and pulled him after her through the rhododendrons. They both had to crouch down to avoid the leaves and branches, and Alan started whining.

166

'This'll get me clothes dirty. You can't take me 'ere.' But he still followed her through the bushes.

'It'll be all right,' Millie said. 'It's not far.' Then she stopped and looked round. 'It's meant to be a surprise,' she said, inspecting the bushes.

'What d'you mean?' Alan said, standing beside her.

'You're not supposed to see it until you get there.' She frowned at the next bush.

'See what?' Alan peered at the bush impatiently. 'I can't see anythin'.'

'That's it,' Millie said. 'They won't come out while you're looking.'

'What'cher talkin' about,' Alan said, perplexed.

'The Club,' Millie said. 'The club people. They don't want you to see it until they're ready.'

'Aren't they ready?' Alan said, surprised, and then he giggled nervously. 'They're expectin' me, aren't they?'

'Oh yes,' Millie said firmly, then she abruptly pulled out of her pocket a large white handkerchief already folded diagonally into a strip. 'I'll blindfold you.' She quickly stepped behind him and lifted up the handkerchief before he fully understood what she was doing, but when the handkerchief touched his face he swung round, knocking into Millie.

'What's this?' he said nervously.

'Ouch,' Millie called out at the same time. 'You've stepped on my toe.'

'Did I?' Alan said contritely.

'Stand still,' Millie ordered. She put the handkerchief again round his face, and he stood meekly unmoving, with his head bowed. She tightened the cloth round his eyes and started working on the knot at the back of his head.

'I can't see,' he wailed in astonishment.

'Wait,' she snapped, concentrating on the knot to make sure that it was a truly firm one. She must not let herself down at this stage. 'It'll be all right, I'm taking you.'

'I can't see where I'm goin'.' He started to whine half-tearfully.

167

'Oh, please be quiet,' Millie said irritably. 'I'm going to lead you.' She tugged the knot tight and stood back, admiring the stretched cloth round his head.

'It 'urts,' he moaned, but he stood still, his head down, his hands behind his back, his knees weakly bent and his mouth pulled open in the beginning of a sob.

'Don't cry,' Millie said, sounding concerned. But, looking at him, she was filled with contempt at his abject meekness, and with her contempt came a delirious overweening sense of power.

'We'll go now,' she said, her voice gurgling with delight, and she took hold of him firmly by his arm. 'You do what I tell you.'

'Don't let me bump into anythin',' he said, sobbing slightly, and he shuffled sideways, following the pull of her hand.

'It'll be all right,' Millie repeated disinterestedly. 'Keep your head down.' She lifted the branch of rhododendron and they shuffled underneath, held close together arm in arm, but she was not so careful with the next branch and it dropped too soon, hitting Alan on his back.

'Ow,' he yelled sharply, jerking forward and shaking Millie.

'Stop it, stop it,' she hissed furiously and gripped his arm with both her hands, holding him still. Then she slowly twisted round and stared out through the remaining branches into the clearing. She could see the three ropes, hanging without any movement in the centre of the clearing, and she could see the metal box, on its side beneath the middle rope, but she could see no sign whatsoever of any of the boys. The clearing appeared to be empty, and she looked round suspiciously, wondering if they had cooked up a trick in her absence.

'What's 'appening',' Alan whispered.

'It's all right,' Millie said grimly. 'They're getting things ready.' Then she added defiantly, 'we don't need them anyway.'

'Who?' Alan said faintly.

'Come on,' Millie replied. She led him carefully out of the bushes and into the clearing, holding his arm with both her hands and treading cautiously. Half-way to the ropes she stopped, as unmistakably ribald noises had started up from behind the bushes.

'Squeak, squeak. Caaaww,' came from a bush on one side of the clearing.

'Miaooow. Miaooow,' came from a bush on the other side, and Millie, swinging round sharply, caught sight of Draper dodging behind the leaves.

'Hooo. Hooo,' came from the first bush, but Millie could see nobody there in the leaves. 'Toowit. Toowit.' She guessed it was Wellington. Alan remained submissively silent, and Millie took him a few steps forward.

'Who's that?' came the clear voice of Fezel from behind the tree trunk.

'Mr. Green's son.' Wellington had to shout from his bush to talk to Fezel across the clearing. Millie felt Alan shiver, but he said nothing and she continued slowly towards the ropes.

'Who?' Fezel repeated.

'Hoooo, hoooo,' Wellington called out, followed by coarse maniacal laughter.

'Hooo, hooo, hooo,' Draper imitated from his side of the clearing.

'Caaawww, caaaww, caaaww,' came from Wellington.

'Oh, shut up,' Fezel shouted, and there was instant silence. Millie watched warily, but nothing more happened, and she let go of Alan to reach out for the box. Then snaps, cracks and crashes, receding from behind the bushes, made it clear that the three boys were running away, and fast, through the grove.

'Where are you,' Alan bleated, but Millie waited until she could no longer hear the boys, and Alan, shuffling in unsteady circles, started his sobbing wails.

'Here,' Millie said, and, grasping the box, she pulled it beneath the end rope. 'You can be quiet now.' She continued to be impelled not only by the urge for action and the sweet taste of power, but also by the obvious impossibility now of turning back. But though she felt let down by the boys, she knew she could go on without them.

'You have to stand on this.' Millie steadied Alan by putting her hands on his shoulders, and then guided him to the box. He followed miserably, sobbing intermittently.

'Kneel on it first,' she ordered, but getting him up on the box proved to be more difficult than she had expected.

'Why, why, why,' he wailed, his knees touching the rusty edge of the box.

'So you can join the Club, so you can get the prize,' Millie said wildly. 'You have to stand up on it, otherwise they won't give it to you. Come on, hurry up.' She pushed first one of his legs and then the other, until he was kneeling, gently sobbing, in the centre of the box. Then she pushed hard at his elbow. 'Stand up now, stand up,' she ordered, and she kept on pushing until he had raised himself clumsily onto his feet.

'There, you're nearly ready now,' she said with satisfaction. The rope, with the lasso noose at the end, hung to one side of his head, and Millie, standing on tiptoe, took hold of the loop and tucked the end under his chin.

'What's that?' Alan gasped out.

'It's all right,' Millie said cheerfully. She pulled the loop backwards, stretching up to bring the rope behind his ears to the back of his head and tugged it slightly as she slipped down on her feet. 'That's your crown,' she cried out. 'You wear that to get the prize.'

Alan opened his mouth and let out a howl, then paused while he took in breath for the next sobbing wail. Tears trickled down his face from beneath the handkerchief blocking his eyes, his head held rigid in the noose while his hands shook against his back and his whole body shuddered from the sobs. Millie noticed that his knees were actually knocking against each other.

'Now jump,' she said and gave a little laugh. She ran back a few paces and drew in her breath with a hiss. 'Jump, jump, jump,' she snarled. She ran to the edge of the clearing and turned back. 'Jump, jump,' she said automatically, although he would not hear her over his cries. Then she flung herself at the rhododendron branches, crashing through the bushes, away from the clearing, away from the pavilion, hearing the pathetic wails until she reached the far end of the grove.

At the edge of the grove she stopped and took stock of her appearance. She straightened her white socks and shook her dress, noticing that one of the pockets was torn, and then brushed her hands fiercely over her hair, making sure that there were no leaves caught in her pigtails. Then, holding her hands composedly in front of her dress, she stepped out onto the front lawn and faced the distant cricket match.

Merryman was the centre of attention, she noticed as she walked carefully across the grass towards the pavilion. Fielders, dotted about in the distance, were waving and pointing and calling out to him, as he stood glumly by the stumps, looking more portly than ever with a loose white coat, a sweater draped round his shoulders and a floppy white hat on his head. At last he held up his hand, and there was cheering and clapping. There was applause from the onlookers too, strung out in a row on deck chairs either side of the pavilion. Millie could just see the flowers on her mother's hat bobbing about as she made encouraging comments to the ladies on each side. The English master stood behind the deck chairs, leaning against the back of one of them where Millie could see pink trousered legs sticking out in front. He was not showing any great interest in the game, and he did not move to join in the applause, nor did he smile as he watched Millie's father walking towards the pavilion. Millie's father, on the other hand, was laughing as he approached the boys of his team. He kept his bat tucked tightly under his arm, while he slipped off his padded gloves, and he moved each leg with an even flick as he lifted the thick white pads on his calves. 'Well done, sir,' the next boy batsman said, clothed ready for the fray, as they passed each other. 'Well done, sir. Good show,' the other boys said, as Millie's father joined them in front of the pavilion.

The junior boys sat on the grass beyond the deck chairs, extending the circle of onlookers. Millie came quite near them on her way to find her place among the staff and visitors. Fezel and Wellington and Draper sat among a group of cricket enthusiasts, relaxed and unperturbed, nodding towards the score-board and

171

pointing to the next batsman. Millie continued down behind the row of deck chairs, looking at the heads sticking up over the tops of the chairs, some identifiable but most of them strangers, some straw hats, some felt hats, some tidy hair, some untidy, some white, some curly and some so small that they were below the tops of the chairs. Millie stopped behind her mother's chair and stood next to the English master.

'Where've you been, Millie,' he said without interest.

Millie's mother twisted round in the chair and held out her arm. 'Oh darling,' she said, smiling. 'There you are. Your father made such a high score.' Her hand fluttered towards the pavilion. 'We must be so proud of him.' She shifted her chair in little jerks to one side. 'Come and sit down on the grass beside me. It's the Head Boy batting now, we'll see how he does.'

Millie squeezed forward between the deck chairs and sat on the ground beside her mother's feet. Her mother was telling the pink-suited sister, in the chair next to her, about the star cricket players of past school teams. The sister was smiling and nodding, and the English master leant forward gloomily. Millie could hear her father's laugh coming from the pavilion, and there was another ripple of applause as the Head Boy hit a boundary on his first ball. Millie looked round at the peaceful scene, everyone happy and contented, joined in a common game right across to the far corners of the field, as far as the eye could reach. The only apparant discord was from the English master behind her, and he was no ally of hers. She picked a blade of grass and thoughtfully put it in her mouth. If only something would happen to change the world completely.

13

Nancy Matters sat by the large toy box in Millie's room, the cupboard door propped open behind the chair, and she lifted up one toy at a time.

'This pop-gun,' Nancy Matters said. 'Do you want to keep this?'

'No,' Millie said. She was sitting at the table, her elbows pushed forward on the top and her head resting in her hands. She looked utterly bored. Nancy Matters dropped the pop-gun into a cardboard box in front of the cupboard and picked out the next toy.

'This drum?' she said, holding it up.

'No,' Millie said.

Nancy Matters rummaged in the box. 'This golliwog?'

'No.' The golliwog dropped into the cardboard box, and the next toy was held up.

'This pistol?'

'No.'

'This doll?'

'No.'

'But it's a pretty doll. Don't be so silly, you must keep something.' Nancy Matters jogged the doll up and down.

'Don't want it,' Millie said.

'All right, if that's how you feel.' Nancy Matters threw the doll into the cardboard box and pursed her lips disdainfully.

'This box of games?' Nancy Matters had to hold up the box with both her hands.

'No,' Millie drawled.

Nancy Matters sighed and put down the games box. Then she held up a net bag of doll's clothes. 'This?'

'No.'

'This puzzle?'

'No.'

'This toy microscope?'

'No.'

'This teddy bear?'

'No.'

'This is ridiculous.' Nancy Matters flung down the teddy bear and stood up. 'Why don't you want to keep any of your toys?'

Millie watched her with amusement. 'Because I don't,' she said, and then sat up straighter. 'But I'll take some of my books with me.'

'Well, you can choose those yourself,' Nancy Matters said crossly. She lifted out the remaining toys and put them with the others in the cardboard box. 'This will make a lovely present,' she said, her voice laced with fury, 'for a poor little girl who has not been as lucky as yourself.' She gestured at the ample room, without looking directly at Millie. 'It's not every little girl who has everything she could want.' She shook her head in disgust. 'There's gratitude for you, I must say.' She finally looked at Millie with a mixture of contempt and curiosity, as if Millie was only half human. 'Whatever made you do such a thing?' she said slowly.

Millie returned her gaze unblinkingly, without attempting to reply. To Millie, the room appeared bleak, with all the words and letters taken from the walls, with her children's posters, illustrations from Alice in Wonderland which she had grown to love, unpinned and taken down, with her miniature animals, her wooden mice and bears and her furry tiger and owls, all removed from along the mantelpiece, her pencils and paper cleared out, her bedside drawer emptied and all her collection of string taken away. It was now nothing to do with her, and she would have none of it.

'Be like that, then, for all I care,' Nancy Matters said with a shake of her head, and set herself in front of the bookcase. The work books were in neat piles, tied up in bundles by subjects, and there remained one row of Millie's books unsorted.

174

'What's this?' Nancy Matters said, picking up an oddly shaped drawing book.

'That's my jometry,' Millie said, getting up quickly. 'I want that.'

Nancy Matters flicked the pages over, watching the haphazard lines and letters flash by. 'Doesn't look sense to me,' she said, giggling.

'You wouldn't understand!' Millie shouted, and she snatched the book out of Nancy Matters' hands and clutched it to her chest. 'It's important.'

Nancy Matters slapped Millie on the side of the head, smartly and firmly, not very hard but enough to startle Millie exceedingly. 'There's no need to behave like that,' Nancy Matters shouted in turn.

'You're not to hit me,' Millie muttered.

'Then you behave properly,' Nancy Matters said, quietening down. She pointed to the row of books. 'Which of these do you want?'

Millie looked at her beloved stories, her source of heavenly worlds, where adventures were exciting and had happy endings, or at any rate the heroes were admired by all even if they ended up dead. 'I want them all,' she said grumpily.

'Oh, my little Miss,' Nancy Matters said with a sneer. 'And where are your manners.' She pointed to a battered suitcase by the wall. 'You can pack them in yourself.' Millie stood still, scowling miserably, holding tight to her drawing book and preparing herself for the next onslaught, and Nancy Matters exploded.

'Well, really, I don't know,' she spluttered. 'What's to be done with you.' She waved her arms helplessly. 'It's no wonder Miss Ellen refused to stay on.' She gave a deep sigh. 'She's well out of it, that's for sure. You're just a . . .' She stopped, lost for words, and scratched her head. 'I know one thing,' she said finally, with a laugh. 'You're a proper little problem. Or better still,' she added, enjoying her own joke, 'a blooming great problem.'

More cheerful now, she pushed the suitcase to the books. 'We

175

must be getting on. You stack in the books as neat as you can,' she said, smiling at last, and she suddenly patted Millie on the head. 'Cheer up, you're not dead yet.'

Millie flinched at first, expecting another slap, but when Nancy Matters laughed again she relaxed and carefully knelt down beside the open suitcase. 'Big ones first,' Nancy Matters said, standing before her and holding open the lid.

Millie placed the drawing book at the bottom of the case and then chose the tallest books to put in next. She gave each one a loving squeeze before laying them down, not knowing when she would see them again. Everything had become uncertain, and there was no corner of security left, like living on top of a shifting pile of sand. She had been told that her suitcases would travel with her, but she could rely on nothing and she must learn to be sufficient with only her head and her hands, and not even string in her pocket.

'You're a regular little bookworm, aren't you,' Nancy Matters said, half mockingly, as she watched Millie pile her books into the suitcase.

'I love my books,' Millie said defensively. There were many of her spheres which she could relinquish, but there remained a few which she must stand up for, and among these the most important were her treasured tales and magic stories. Most of them were only half remembered from when they were read to her, but she was filling in the gaps and the original sources must be protected with care.

'Well done,' Nancy Matters said when Millie fitted the last small books down the side of the case. 'Now, stand up. I want to make sure you're tidy.' Millie wearily stood up and waited. There was no point any more in disobedience, not for a long time to come. She had chanced playing her Grand Master Plan, and it had very nearly succeeded. She had done the best she could, to the utmost of her abilities, given her age and size and sex and learning. There had been no mistake in her part of the Plan, no clumsy fault or miscalculation, and only one small stage had remained between the execution of the Plan and its Final

Success. Why had Alan not jumped? Why had he stood there, hands tied, eyes bandaged, head in noose, and wailed and not jumped? It must be, Millie reasoned, because she was a little girl, and little girls did not have enough authority. If she had been bigger, and a boy, she would have been obeyed implicitly. Now she would grow more, indeed she was growing all the time without doing anything about it, so that was taken care of. There was not much she could do about her sex, except compensate for being a girl by being extra stout and cross, like Cook or Matron who were both always obeyed. She would practise being stern and frowning, and remember to eat as much as she could.

Nancy Matters twitched at Millie's dress and smoothed down her hair. 'You don't look too bad,' she said smugly. 'Now pull up your socks.' Millie lifted a foot in turn and gave a token tug at the short white socks. 'A bit better than that,' Nancy Matters said, triumphant that Millie so readily did as she was told. 'You can look pretty if you try.' Millie bent down and pulled and twisted uselessly at the socks. It would be a waste of time to argue with a woman such as Nancy Matters, or to even try to explain the pointlessness of being pretty. There were some endeavours on which it was not worth wasting the breath.

'Ready at last,' Nancy Matters said, looking with satisfaction at Millie. 'Now you can go down and say goodbye to Mr. and Mrs. Hamble.' She put her hand on Millie's shoulder and walked with her to the door of Millie's room. 'They're expecting you in the pantry. Run along now.' She patted Millie on the back. 'Be a good girl, and come back upstairs when you're told to.' She smiled at Millie, and gave a little wave of her hand as Millie left the room.

Although Millie said nothing and kept up her frowning, she was nevertheless glad to leave her room, where she had been confined for hours, and then days until they had decided what to do with her. She was allowed out into the house once the holidays had started, but all the fun of adventure had gone out of the place now that there was no point in being naughty, and it was a dull house when there were no evil deeds to search out. She

177

had stayed in her room voluntarily most of the time, staring dreamily out of her window or painstakingly reading her adventure stories. At times she had felt like an animal on display when various members of the staff had casually arrived, ostensibly on a mission of kindliness but Millie had sensed the purient curiosity beneath their idle chatter. They had looked at her sideways and grinned uneasily, and talked of the school fête. The English master had been the only one to refer directly to any part of the whole affair or to Alan himself. 'I am not surprised,' he had said viciously, looking straight at Millie. 'And it is just like you to pick on someone less advantaged and then believe that you can kick them around to your heart's content.' Millie had squirmed and remained silent, which had drawn more fire. 'You spend your time plotting, I can see,' he had said, jabbing a finger at her forehead. 'You have one thought in that mind of yours, and one thought only, and that is mischief, how to make mischief.' Millie had blinked, but bravely kept her gaze on him. 'You are an evil little girl,' he had ended with, and Millie had pondered his words in the quiet of the evening, when she lay in bed and stared at the blank walls of her room. There would be others like the English master, and more words would be slung at her, but they were not her true adversaries. The English master recognized her for what she was worth, whether it was bad or good, and he was not set up in opposition to her, ready to engage in battle. At times he hardly seemed to care, and in certain circumstances, Millie thought with a giggle, she would not be surprised to find him as an ally after all.

Confrontation had not been possible for her father. He had stood in front of her, deflated, tired, distant, and he had stared incongruously at the lampshade in the centre of her room, with its pictures of a grinning and dancing Mickey Mouse. Millie had waited patiently for many silent minutes while he chose his words. Eventually he told her that she was to be sent away to a school, where she would live, and have her lessons, and she would have holidays with her parents. A boarding school, Millie thought to herself, and why had he not called it that straight out?

178

They were very strict about behaviour, he had gone on to say, and she would have to learn to be good, and be good in the holidays too. It would not be difficult, Millie thought, to bide her time and show good behaviour until she was really bigger and cleverer. It gave excellent schooling, he had said, the lessons were thorough with a wide range of subjects and she would learn a lot. Millie smiled with pleasure at the chance to increase her knowledge, and her father, looking baffled and dejected, had left her.

The Hambles were the only members of staff whom she had not seen. Neither of them had been up to visit her, and she had not considered it politic to wander into the pantry without invitation. But now, officially summoned by them, she was curious to see how changed the pantry atmosphere would be.

She noticed a difference at once when Hamble did not offer her a seat but stood with his chin on his chest, arms crossed, scowling at her reprovingly. 'Tut, tut, tut,' he said slowly, and then he bent forward and whispered each word separately. 'How could you do such a thing?' He drew in a deep breath as he straightened up. 'Tut, tut, tut, tut,' he repeated, shaking his head from side to side, and he continued to shake his head in meaningful silence.

Millie stood abashed, picking uncomfortably at the pockets of her dress. She needed a cue to know how to behave next, but she sensed that Hamble cared more deeply for her than anyone throughout the whole school, and she waited for some cheerfulness to break through.

'You may as well have some tea,' Mrs. Hamble said sadly. She was standing at the cupboard with her back to Millie, taking out tea cups.

'Oh, oh, oh,' Hamble said. 'But she doesn't deserve a biscuit.'

'No good will come of starving her,' Mrs. Hamble said, as she laid out three cups on the table.

'Aha,' Hamble said. 'Who can tell. Maybe she's had too much of sweet cakes, and not enough of love.'

Mrs. Hamble smiled knowingly. She took out of the cupboard

179

a plate piled high with jam doughnuts and chocolate eclairs. Millie gasped as the delicacies were put on the table. These were her avowed favourites, and she realized that Mrs. Hamble must have chosen them specially for her. She felt most peculiar, like crying, but this was silly because why cry at doughnuts?

Hamble lurched forward clumsily and flung his arms round Millie, lifting her off her feet. She could feel his warm face against hers and his breath on her neck.

'Oh, oh, my Missie Millie,' he moaned and rocked backwards and forwards, holding Millie tight as he swayed. 'Whatever is to become of you?' Millie's face was pressed helplessly into his coat collar, as he swayed and moaned. 'Such a carry on, such a to do. Oh, how could it happen.' He abruptly jerked back his head and grinned at Millie as she rested her cheek on his shoulder. 'So what shall we do with you? Eh? Eh?' He swung her down and stepped back, smiling at her with his head on one side. 'Shall we punish you with bread and water?' Then he bent over and whispered. 'Or will you have a good tea before you go?'

Millie laughed with relief to find herself in such a haven of abundance, and strange little tears crept out of the corner of her eyes. She sniffed a few times and searched in her pocket for her missing handkerchief.

'Come and sit down,' Mrs. Hamble said, placing the teapot on the table. 'It's all ready.'

Hamble waved his arm towards the table. 'My Lady Missie Millie, your place awaits you,' he said grandly, and gave a small bow.

Millie laughed again, and, sniffing and smiling, she went to the table and sat down opposite Mrs. Hamble. 'Help yourself,' Mrs. Hamble said, pushing the plate towards her, and Millie took a sticky doughnut and bit into it carefully.

Hamble, busy at the cupboard behind Millie, took out the sugar bowl and swung it with a flourish over Millie's shoulder. 'We don't forget your sweet tooth, either,' he said delightedly, placing it on the table in front of her.

'Don't encourage her too much,' Mrs. Hamble said, looking at

180

Millie who was eating her doughnut with her chin close to her rosebud plate in order to keep the crumbs off the tablecloth.

Millie felt that something was required of her. 'Thank you very much, Mr. Hamble,' she said between bites of the doughnut, and then she caught Mrs. Hamble's eye. 'Thank you Mrs. Hamble for the doughnuts,' she added clearly.

Hamble startled her by laughing uproariously, as he stood behind her chair. 'Don't mock her manners,' Mrs. Hamble objected fiercely. 'You'll make her worse, not better.' She poured tea into a rosebud cup. 'Here, take your tea. You should set her a good example, that's what she needs.' She primly put the cup down in front of Hamble as he sat at the head of the table. 'Her manners are all she has left to her name.'

'Millie knows my little ways, don't you my Missie?' Hamble said, smiling at Millie.

'That's one good thing that's come out of it,' Mrs. Hamble went on. 'She'll be away from the boys who lead her astray.'

'What?' Hamble said sharply. 'You can't believe it was the boys who taught her to . . . to . . . .' He hesitated. 'Taught her to do what she did.' He frowned seriously as he sipped his tea.

'Who can tell,' Mrs. Hamble said smugly. 'Who knows what ideas go into that head of hers.' She examined Millie from across the table. 'She picks up things from here and from there, things she shouldn't always be listening to.' She looked from Millie to Hamble. 'They get mixed up in her mind.'

'That's rubbish,' Hamble said firmly. 'Her mind's as clear as a bell.' He looked thoughtfully at Millie. 'She's clever enough, we all know that.' He stared at the strands of curly hair which were falling over her face, already slightly out of control. 'I do believe, if you ask me, the trouble is,' he turned to his wife, 'lack of supervision, that's the cause of the trouble.' They nodded wisely at each other.

'Lack of supervision,' she repeated quietly. 'No discipline, left to run wild.'

'You'll find that's where the trouble lies,' he said, and helped himself to a doughnut. 'Not enough care and attention.' They

181

both examined Millie again.

Millie clung to the piece of information that manners were important. 'Please, Mrs. Hamble,' she said precisely. 'May I have an éclair?'

Mrs. Hamble smiled and handed her the plate. 'There now,' she said sweetly. 'She wants attention, you see?'

Hamble smiled happily. 'Eat up, eat up,' he said to Millie. 'Have as much as you want. There's no need to hold back here.' He attacked his own doughnut.

'By rights,' Mrs. Hamble said, pouring out more tea into her cup, 'it's for the parents to provide the care and attention.'

'Ah,' Hamble said, jabbing the air with his doughnut. 'Now you're talking.' He chewed another mouthful in thoughtful silence.

'But if the heart is not willing,' Mrs. Hamble said with a meaningful sigh. 'Or if the heart is given elsewhere, then what can you expect?'

'That's a point.' Hamble suddenly leant over to Millie. 'Did you see your mother before she went away?'

'No,' Millie said, surprised.

'She wouldn't have done,' Mrs. Hamble said indignantly. 'Her mother in a state like that.' She re-filled Hamble's cup. 'They did get her away quickly, I must say. Taken ill one day, gone the next.'

'Shock,' Hamble said. 'It was the shock that did it. I've seen them like it on the battlefield, running all round and not knowing ...'

'They called it a nervous breakdown,' Mrs. Hamble interrupted loudly, shouting at her husband over the tea cups.

'It's all the same thing,' he said, glaring at his wife.

'It is not the same thing,' she shouted emphatically.

'They all go nutty the same,' he shouted back at her. There was an awkward silence, and then Mrs. Hamble smiled at Millie and lifted the plate. 'Would you like another cake?' she said, leaning forward attentively.

'Yes, please,' Millie said, and took another éclair. She had in

182

fact seen her mother on the evening after the fateful day, but no one had known that Millie had crept out of her room and peered over the bannisters, and it was best kept a total secret. She had been attracted by the strange animal-like cries, repeated piercingly over and over again, and she had peered down into the hall to see a flurry of activity. Her mother was in the centre of it all, her full skirt sweeping round as she twisted and turned and one neat court shoe fell off as she kicked her legs. Her hair was completely loose and it swept wildly over her face and shoulders, sometimes smothering her cries and at other times, when she flung back her head, revealing a strained and distraught face, her eyes and mouth wider open than Millie had ever seen them. She was surrounded by men whom Millie did not know, some of them in white shirts with their sleeves rolled up, though she did recognize her father, standing at the edge of the group in his usual jacket and calling out instructions ineffectually. The men were calling out instructions too, some to each other and some to her mother, and they all had their arms raised, trying to grasp different parts of her mother as she flailed and twisted. Her mother defied them all for a long time, considering the number of opponents around her, and she seemed to be sustained in her frenzied ducks and kicks and punches by her repeated shuddering cries. For the first time Millie was whole-heartedly on the side of her mother, hoping against hope that her mother would escape the clutching hands and be forever free and undefeated and never ever giving herself up.

But abruptly the cries stopped, and her mother crumpled onto the floor, and one of the men immediately covered her tightly with a sheet, and the others held her firmly from every side. She lay there whimpering like a frightened animal. Her father looked over the men's shoulders, still giving orders, and they slowly lifted her up. It took six agitated men, with her father following behind, to carry her mother out of the front door. Millie told herself that her mother might be subjected to endless awful indignities, but she was sure she would never give in, her mother would remain steadfast to the end and never betray her own true self.

Millie licked at the cream squeezing out of the end of her éclair and watched Mrs. Hamble cutting a doughnut neatly into mouthful-sized pieces.

'Poor woman,' Mrs. Hamble said. 'She'll never be the same again.'

'You're wrong there,' Hamble said. 'She'll be right as rain by next term, just as if nothing had happened, you mark my words.'

Mrs. Hamble haughtily ignored him and attended to Millie. 'Would you like some more tea, Millie? Pass me your cup.'

'Yes, please, Mrs. Hamble,' Millie said dutifully, pushing her cup over. The tea party was not being such fun as the plate of delicacies had promised, and her éclair had lost its attraction. She turned to Hamble, mutely appealing for cheerful reassurance.

'There now, my Missie Millie,' Hamble said, responding at once. 'Cheer up, my girl.' He leant over and patted her hand. 'There's no need to look so glum. Worse can happen.'

'What a thing to say,' Mrs. Hamble said, outraged, putting down Millie's cup with a clatter.

Hamble laughed, giving Millie's hand a squeeze. 'It's not the end of the world. You'll see, it won't be such a bad place after all.'

'What place?' Millie said, puzzled and not entirely reassured.

'Why, the place they're sending you to,' Hamble said reasonably. 'It's said they teach you a lot there.'

'It's strict, though,' Mrs. Hamble said grimly. 'They'll use the cane.'

'Not on girls, they won't,' Hamble said, turning crossly to his wife.

'There'll be punishments, that's certain,' Mrs. Hamble said righteously.

'My Missie Millie can be good when she likes,' Hamble said, leaning back in his chair and looking thoughtfully at Millie.

'I like my lessons,' Millie said, feeling that it was her turn to reassure Hamble. She smiled at him eagerly. 'I'll work hard, and I'll learn all my new subjects.'

184

'I've been told,' Hamble said, rocking forward and dropping his voice to a whisper, 'that there's a heated swimming pool, and tennis courts, and if you're very good,' he tapped Millie's arm with his finger, 'there are horses you can ride.'

'I don't believe that,' Mrs. Hamble said stuffily.

Hamble jerked his head round. 'Why not?' He scowled at his wife. 'Why not? They have to take their turn in the stables, so I've been told, so why can't they take their turn on the horses? Where's the point in horses, I ask you, if they're never ridden? Answer me that, then, answer me that.'

Mrs. Hamble sighed and stared into her empty tea cup. 'There's no need to take on so. You don't set a very good example for Millie, I must say.' She slowly turned her head to look at him with contempt.

He stared steadily at his wife, and they glowered at each other for a moment in silence. Then he lifted his finger and pointed it at her like a gun. 'I'll tell you one thing,' he said slowly. 'You can keep your governesses and your grand drawing rooms and your lunch at the master's table. When it comes to bringing up young girls, she'll learn more here,' he banged the table with his finger, 'whatever she sees or hears in this room.'

'I know that,' Mrs. Hamble said, unrepentant. 'I've said all along that she should be kept away from the boys.'

'It's not the boys,' Hamble said and gave a heavy sigh of despair. 'The masters are almost a worse influence.'

'That's what I said,' Mrs. Hamble said indignantly. 'No home life, I told you this would happen with no proper home life for her.'

Hamble laughed and slapped the table. 'So we agree on something, then.' He continued to laugh contentedly, looking round from his position at the head of the table.

Millie decided that she was learning nothing new at all in the room that afternoon, and she slid down off her chair. 'Please may I go now?' she said, with a tinge of regret that the Hambles had not quite lived up to her expectations.

She caused an immediate stir, as both the Hambles stood up in a fluster. 'Oh dear,' Mrs. Hamble said vaguely and looked at the plate of remaining éclairs.

'So it's goodbye to our Missie Millie,' Hamble said with a gasp.

'I'm sure it's all for the best,' Mrs. Hamble said uncertainly.

'It won't be the same with you gone,' Hamble said sadly, and Millie laughed at him for his truthfulness.

'There's my girl,' he said, surprised by her laughter. 'So you can put a brave face on it when you try.'

'She's always been a brave little girl', Mrs. Hamble said, smiling sweetly at Millie. 'You're a plucky girl, I can say that.'

'Now, just for us,' Hamble poked his head forward and whispered, 'be a good girl.' Millie nodded at him sadly.

'Oh, my goodness,' Mrs. Hamble said, twisting round to the cupboard. 'The present.'

'Oh, yes, yes,' Hamble said, looking from side to side. 'The present.'

'We nearly forgot to give her the present,' Mrs. Hamble said, poking around inside the cupboard.

'It's over here,' Hamble said, going to the cupboard at the other side of the room. Millie waited by the table in the centre of the room while the Hambles fussed about at either side. She could not imagine what they would have chosen for her, but she hoped that it did not replace any of the toys which she had so relentlessly succeeded in discarding. She did not think it likely that they would choose a book, and she wondered if he would give her one of his army relics, a gun, perhaps, or a medal. She would like that.

'Here it is,' Hamble said, and he drew out a square parcel, wrapped in pretty coloured paper.

'Oooo,' Millie said with pleasure and excitement. 'Can I open it now?'

'Oh, no,' Mrs. Hamble said. 'You take it with you, and you can open it when you get to your new home.'

'It'll be a surprise for you,' Hamble said, leaning down to give her the present. Millie took the parcel and held it by the edges, gently feeling to see what shape it was inside. She realized immediately that it was a book, recognizing the hard cover projecting beyond the flat pages, and a large book too.

'Oh, thank you very much,' Millie said sincerely. 'Oh, thank you Mrs. Hamble, thank you so much, Hamble.' How could she let them know that she really meant it this time? 'I mean it this time, really I do.'

The Hambles both laughed delightedly, and Mrs. Hamble came round the table. 'It's to remind you of us,' she said, and she bent down delicately and gave Millie a slow soft kiss on her cheek. Millie was unused to the feel of Mrs. Hamble's face, and she was surprised at its hairiness. She watched it carefully while Mrs. Hamble stood up and smiled..

'Goodbye, Mrs. Hamble,' Millie said, now sorry that she was leaving when there was more to find out about Mrs. Hamble.

'You won't forget,' Hamble whispered in his turn, 'to come back and visit us, from time to time.' He held Millie by her shoulders and looked at her searchingly, his face close to hers, and then he gave a noisy kiss on each of her cheeks. 'Give us a thought, now and again,' he added, laughing.

Millie laughed with him, holding her present in her arms. 'I can write you a letter, can't I?' she said proudly.

'Why, of course,' Hamble said, standing up and stepping back to look at Millie. 'My Missie Millie can write now, as well as read.' He nodded seriously. 'You're a clever girl.'

'You can let us know how you're getting on,' Mrs. Hamble said.

Millie smiled and nodded and walked sideways to the door, watching the Hambles as they stood helplessly by the table. They seemed rooted in the pantry, unable to reach beyond the world of the school for all their superior knowledge, and it was Millie who was venturing forth. They stood unmoving, their hands by their sides, looking on resignedly. Millie felt a sense of exhilaration at the thought that there was nothing to stop her now, and she waved happily.

'Goodbye, goodbye,' she said at the door. Mrs. Hamble blew her a kiss and gave a little wave in return.

'Remember,' Hamble said in an unexpectedly firm and loud voice. 'Be a good girl.' He spoke sternly, without a hint of his usual jollity, and Millie found this unpleasantly alarming.

'Yes,' she said respectfully. 'Yes, I'll be good.' Could she count this as a white lie?

'Promise me now,' Hamble said with a return to cheerfulness. 'Yes, oh yes,' Millie said gaily, and retreated through the door.

'Goodbye, my Missie Millie,' she heard him call.

'Goodbye, goodbye,' she called out as she walked slowly backwards down the corridor. 'Goodbye.' She turned to push open the green baize door and she walked silently across the hall and half-way up the stairs. There she stopped and looked through the bannisters, realizing that everywhere was silent and empty, and she was completely alone.

She sat down on the stair and rested the present on her lap, feeling all round the edges of the paper. Since it was a book she would pack it in the case with the others, but it would make sense to find out what book it was before she put it away. There was no reason to keep the wrapping paper on, in fact it would be a nuisance in the case and might get torn anyway. She pulled gently at the coloured string, tied in a neat bow, and found that it came undone easily. It was her book, after all, now that it had been given to her, and it was a silly idea to wait to see what book it was. She pulled off the string and carefully opened the ends of the paper, trying not to let it tear. It was a heavy book, and it would surely provide a lot of exciting reading. Would it have stories of Hamble's battles? Probably not, as Mrs. Hamble would stop that. But there were plenty of other good stories. She caught sight of a black cover as she lifted open the paper, which seemed a gloomy start, and it was discouraging to have no picture on the outside, but no doubt there were illustrations inside. She took the book out of the paper and held it in both hands, examining it on all sides. She noticed that the edges of the pages were coloured gold, giving three narrow gold sides to the book when it was closed, which was excitingly special. Could it contain stories of Kings and Queens? She opened it at random

188

and saw at once that the lines of print did not run across the page from one side to the other but were in two columns on each page, and in lots of short paragraphs. Her heart sank, as she had seen this before, always in authoritarian circumstances, and she quickly turned to the very front of the book with foreboding. Inside the front cover, on the fly leaf, was a handwritten message, to herself because she recognized the words 'To Millie Newman,' and then it went on 'with loving.' She would work out the rest of the words later, as the writing was not so clear, but it was obviously from the Hambles. She turned the next page, which was disappointingly thin and flimsy, and then she came to the title page, and there it was, written at the top, 'The Holy Bible,' in black letters.

Millie stood up, furious. What use was this to her? What use to her was the very set of rules used by her enemies to trap and quell her? How could this heavy black book show her the delicate path through the minefields laid by authority? How could the Hambles of all people, supposed to be her best friends and her allies, have fobbed her off with such a joyless gift? How could they have acted so stuffily? How could they presume to tell her what to do and to try to infiltrate her moral life? Why did she have to be good? She kicked at the coloured wrapping paper on the stair, again and again, until it lay in a crumpled ball against the bannisters. She ignored the coloured string and went up a step towards her room.

There was no question of her abandoning her naughtiness. She had spent far too much work on it to turn her back on it now. She had given it her concentration, and she had taken a great deal of time and trouble over it, and above all she had blessed it with her care and attention as a proper parent should. Now it was just beginning to blossom and to show its manifold potential, and it was starting to give her confidence in return. She could not let it down now. It would grow with her, and become big and strong when she became a woman.

She took another step up. When she grew up she would be a General and she would have hundreds of soldiers under her command, and they would all have guns, and she would send them all into battle, shooting and killing as they went, and she would have millions of bombs raining down from aeroplanes and exploding houses and cities. She would be a Prime Minister and it would be she who ordered people about and made the rules, and it would be she who told her enemies what to do and kept them in their places. She would be a Judge with wavy hair and she would decide who was good and who was bad, and she would send them all to prison and condemn them to death. She would be a Priest and send people to hellfire and bottomless pits and endless torture and eternal damnation. She would be all these rolled into one, she decided as she walked up the stairs, and she would rule the world, single-handed, alone, and for ever naughty. She tossed back her curls and held her head high as she returned to her room, armed and prepared for her life of growing adventures.